THE GAME MASTERS OF GARDEN PLACE

a gift from

HARBOR
SPRINGS
FESTIVAL
OF THE
book

Inspiring Readers
of All Ages &
Celebrating the
Culture of Books
in a Beautiful
Part of the World

| 2019 | HSFOTB.ORG

Also by Denis Markell

Click Here to Start
The Ghost in Apartment 2R

THE GAME MASTERS OF GARDEN PLACE

DENIS MARKELL

A YEARLING BOOK

Sale of this book without a front cover may be unauthorized. If the book is coverless, it may have been reported to the publisher as "unsold or destroyed" and neither the author nor the publisher may have received payment for it.

This is a work of fiction. Names, characters, places, and incidents either are the product of the author's imagination or are used fictitiously. Any resemblance to actual persons, living or dead, events, or locales is entirely coincidental.

Text copyright © 2018 by Denis Markell
Cover art copyright © 2018 by Octavi Navarro

All rights reserved. Published in the United States by Yearling, an imprint of Random House Children's Books, a division of Penguin Random House LLC, New York. Originally published in hardcover in the United States by Delacorte Press, an imprint of Random House Children's Books, a division of Penguin Random House LLC, New York, in 2018.

Yearling and the jumping horse design are registered trademarks of Penguin Random House LLC.

Visit us on the Web! rhcbooks.com

Educators and librarians, for a variety of teaching tools, visit us at RHTeachersLibrarians.com

The Library of Congress has cataloged the hardcover edition of this work as follows:
Name: Markell, Denis, author.
Title: The game masters of Garden Place / Denis Markell.
Description: First edition. | New York : Delacorte Press, [2018] |
Summary: "When five sixth-graders accidentally summon warriors from their favorite role-playing game to Brooklyn, they are taken on a wild adventure that tests their wits and their friendships"—Provided by publisher.
Identifiers: LCCN 2017024552 | ISBN 978-1-101-93191-2 (hc) |
ISBN 978-1-101-93193-6 (glb) | ISBN 978-1-101-93192-9 (el)
Subjects: | CYAC: Fantasy games—Fiction. | Role playing—Fiction. | Adventure and adventurers—Fiction. | Friendship—Fiction. | Supernatural—Fiction. | Brooklyn (New York, N.Y.)—Fiction.
Classification: LCC PZ7.M339453 Gam 2018 | DDC [Fic]—dc23

ISBN 978-1-101-93194-3 (pbk.)

Printed in the United States of America
10 9 8 7 6 5 4 3 2 1
First Yearling Edition 2019

Random House Children's Books supports the First Amendment and celebrates the right to read.

To Jamie, my favorite game master,
whose great adventure is only beginning

THE DEPTHS OF MORGORATH

Ba-doom. Ba-doom. Ba-doom.

Deep beneath the mountain Morgorath, the stones of the ancient temple echoed with the pounding of the war drums of the Kreel army. It was rumored that the Kreel covered their shields with the skins of their defeated enemies and wore their skulls as trophies.

The group would learn soon enough.

Like a demonic heartbeat, the pulse continued, first barely sensed in the distance but getting ever closer, bringing with it the death and desecration known and feared by all throughout the lands of Demos.

Bram Quickfoot twirled two small daggers between his fingers. One had a bone-white handle, the other a handle of the blackest ebony. The little halfling's eyes were gleaming. "Salt and Pepper are eager for the fight."

The dwarf cleric Torgrim tutted. "Patience, rogue. Don't wish violence on us too early." Then he gathered himself, closed his eyes, and began to chant a spell, calling on the god of protection.

Towering over the cleric, Jandia Ravenhelm unsheathed her two-handed broadsword. "May your prayers protect us." Her muscles rippled as she cut the air with the giant blade.

The soft strumming of a harp filled the temple as the sounds of the bard Mirak's ancient war song began. "The Kreel will fall upon thy sword / Thus have the gods foretold." The song was welcome, as it always seemed to bring added courage to the listeners.

The clamor from the advancing Kreel horde was deafening now, almost upon them.

The four took their positions in view of the temple entrance. Nimbly, Bram leapt up to a rocky ledge above the entrance, where the cunning rogue could choose his targets from the shadows. The cleric finished his oath and pressed his back against the left wall, his massive dwarvish war hammer in hand now, while the bard took position opposite him, calmly stringing her longbow. She grunted softly, feeling the beastly nature of her orc mother rising within her. In quieter times, she would let her human father's gentler qualities prevail, but this was battle. Jandia Ravenhelm pulled herself up to a rocky outcropping directly above the opening, ready to drop upon the heads of the Kreel as they entered.

One remained exposed, kneeling and murmuring to himself. Gerontius Darksbane, wizard of the fourth order, held an orb before him that pulsed with energy, emitting a steady glow. At his waist, still in its scabbard, was his elvish blade.

Within moments, the Kreel burst into the great room, chanting war cries and thirsting for battle.

Calmly, the wizard Darksbane raised his head. He uttered one word.

"Sakanta-sh'ia!"

Fire burst from his fingers, engulfing the entire front line of the Kreel. Those behind felt first the arrows of Mirak the bard, released in a deadly precision. Jandia nodded to Bram, and they fell from above together, hacking through Kreel mail as if it were paper.

Victory did not take long.

As the adventurers stood panting, there was a darkening at the entrance to the temple. They beheld a sight that had broken the spirit of countless warriors before them: the Komach'Kreel, a monster the Kreel priests had torn from the Abyss.

"So it does exist," gasped Torgrim.

"It would appear so, yes," chuckled Bram as he pulled Salt and Pepper from the rib cage of one of the Kreel dead.

Standing a full twelve feet tall, with a whipping tail and fangs dripping with poison, the Komach'Kreel was legendary but almost never seen.

It took the desecration of the temple to bring him to the adventurers, and it would take all their combined powers to bring him down.

As they faced the demonspawn, Jandia Ravenhelm spoke. "Guys, I gotta go."

Bram's jaw dropped in annoyance. "What? You can't just leave!"

"Look, my mom just texted me," said Jandia, sheathing her massive sword.

"Can't she wait a few minutes?" pleaded Darksbane as he plopped down on the floor. "We just met the Komach'Kreel!"

Jandia rolled her eyes. "Are you kidding? She's double-parked. She would literally kill me."

Torgrim grinned and planted his ax in the skull of a nearby Kreel. "She wouldn't *literally* kill you."

Mirak skipped over to Jandia. "Can you drop me? My mom isn't coming until five."

"Sure, of course. Duh," the barbarian warrior replied.

Torgrim sighed. "Well, I guess that's it, then. So we'll pick this up where we left off next weekend?"

PART ONE

THE HEIGHTS OF BROOKLYN

Ralph Peter Ginzberg sighed again as he began to put away the papers, pencils, dice, and other Reign of Dragons paraphernalia. He and his friends had been playing the game every weekend during the school year for the last three years.

Jojo had already zipped her warm-up jacket and was looking for her backpack among the pile of coats and book bags by the front door. She was the only one who hadn't answered.

"You'll be here next week, right, Jojo?" he called after her.

Jojo answered without looking directly at him. She was doing that a lot these days. Ever since she'd joined the sixth-grade gymnastics team, things had changed. "I'm not sure. I mean, we might have a meet or something. Or practice."

Noel Carrington looked up from his gaming magazine. Ralph remembered when all he read were Reign of Dragons rule books and fantasy novels. These days he seemed to be more into the newest thing for his gaming console. "You have to be here. We just met the Komach'Kreel!"

There was the beep of a horn, and Jojo looked out the window of the brownstone's garden-level front room. She waved at the car idling outside. "I gotta go. Perseph, are you coming?"

"Yes!" Persephone Chang heaved her knapsack onto her back. She didn't have any problem finding it in the pile. Between the sparkly *Hamilton* and *Wicked* stickers splayed across it, the plush Simba on the strap, and the gigantic size, it was impossible to miss. It was so large that when she wore it, she looked like a walking backpack with two tiny feet attached.

"Ready to go / To face my fate / The world outside / Will know me!" Persephone sang as she joined Jojo.

The rest gritted their teeth. It wasn't that Persephone had a bad voice—on the contrary, she had an amazing voice. It was especially cool hearing all that sound coming out of such a small body. The first dozen or so times she'd sung this particular song, it was enjoyable, but she had been singing it nonstop for weeks now.

Ralph went to open the door to let the girls out.

"You have to come," Ralph persisted.

"What's the big deal?" Jojo snapped, her soccer bag socking him in the gut as she pushed past him. "Someone else can play Jandia if I'm not here."

"That's ridiculous!" Noel said. "You have to play Jandia! No one is as bloodthirsty or fearless as you!"

Persephone looked at her friend as she joined her in the doorway. "That is totally true, Jojo." Her eyes widened. "Wait! I didn't say goodbye to Cammi!"

Cameron Sprague had remained silent during all this, which was typical. Persephone rushed over and hugged him. "Do you need a ride too? We can squeeze together."

"That's okay," Cammi said in a small voice. "My mom is coming to get me in an hour."

"We can call her," Persephone said, "and she can pick you up at my house! Or maybe we can have a sleepover!"

Persephone certainly wouldn't have invited any other boy in their grade, but Cammi was different. Most of his friends were girls, and he often spent the night with Persephone or Jojo when his mom and grandmother were working late.

"No, that's all right," Cammi insisted. "She said she'd come."

Ralph noticed that Persephone was whispering something in Cammi's ear. He nodded.

Just like a wizard, Ralph thought. Cammi loved secrets. Wizards were like that, keeping to themselves, filled with secret knowledge.

"But you're coming next week, right?" Noel yelled to Jojo from the couch.

"I said I don't know!" Jojo yelled back from the door. "Now can we go?" Her voice sounded as tight as her ponytail, pulled back for sports.

Persephone ran to the door, caroming off a few walls like a pinball on her way out.

No one at St. Anselm's School had more energy than Perseph. Ralph never understood how she was able to sit still during the three hours they normally took to play their adventure every Saturday. Okay, mostly sit still. She did have a habit of breaking into song or dancing around the room. Of course she'd picked a bard. Bards sang magical songs that cast powerful spells on the enemy—that role had Persephone's name written all over it.

Ralph turned back to Noel and Cammi once the girls were gone.

Cammi looked at the floor. "Um, Persephone reminded me to let you know that the play might be starting Saturday rehearsals in a few weeks."

"Are you kidding me?" Ralph said, a little louder than he meant to.

"We're not sure!" Cammi answered quickly. "That's why we didn't want to, you know, say anything until it was for certain."

Ralph stared at Cammi. Saturdays had been their day for so long that this was hard to process. "You guys too?"

"We'll be here next week," Cammi promised quickly. "She just wanted me to warn you about . . . later. . . . And it would just be for a week or two. . . ."

Ralph slumped down on the couch next to Noel. "Boy, Jojo really doesn't seem to be as into the game as she used to be."

"You think?" laughed Noel, grabbing the last of the chips from the bowl Ralph's parents always left for them. "Maybe you should roll for a perception check."

This was an inside joke among the hard-core players of Reign of Dragons, or RoD, as they called it. In the game, whenever you wanted to do anything, whether it was looking around a room for potential traps or bringing your sword down on a fearsome demon, you had to roll the dice. The higher you rolled, the greater your chances of success.

Ralph didn't need to roll the dice to see what was happening around him. It was clear that the game was changing.

2

THE DAWN OF THE REIGN OF DRAGONS

It all started because no one could think of what to do for Ralph's tenth birthday.

His parents had been brainstorming for an hour. Being creative types who worked together producing commercials and promotional films for large corporations, they debated the issue like they were spitballing a commercial pitch, throwing around ideas. Ralph had heard them do this hundreds of times, trying to find something that would "grab" the client and nab them the job. Now they were trying to come up with something that hadn't been done yet.

Noel had had an amazing science-themed party that year, which made sense since his dad worked in a robotics lab.

Jojo's party had been at Prospect Park, near her home, where the kids played games of all kinds. It didn't matter if it was tag or football; somehow Jojo managed to beat everyone, even the largest and sportiest boys.

Persephone and Cammi, as was their tradition, had shared

a party, since their birthdays were so close. Also as was the tradition, all the guests had been roped into creating an original play about twin princesses. Persephone played one, and Cammi, with his long, flowing blond hair, had opted to play the other. His friends were totally cool with this. It was just accepted as part of his wonderful and funny self. As usual, it was quite a production, complete with costumes (it didn't hurt that Cammi's grandmother worked as a seamstress on the costumes of Broadway's biggest shows).

Considering how different the kids were, it was odd that they'd stayed friends. But they had met in kindergarten, when sometimes all it took to become best buddies was sharing a snack or playing pretend for an afternoon. As they moved onto elementary school it just seemed natural to continue to have playdates and celebrate birthdays together, especially since all the parents had become friends as well.

Having exhausted their ideas for Ralph's party (that one was too expensive; this one was too close to what they had done two years ago), his parents were more than receptive when Ralph's babysitter Declan spoke up.

Declan pushed his hair back with his hand. Like everything about Declan, his hair was just cool enough without trying too hard. Ralph knew that all the other families referred to him as the "hipster" babysitter because he was a deejay in his spare time.

"Have you ever heard of Reign of Dragons?" he had asked Ralph's parents.

Ralph's father looked like he was trying hard not to smile. "Sure, that's been around since I was a teenager. I never played it, though. The only ones who did were—"

Ralph's mom cleared her throat loudly. "We're familiar with it."

Declan nodded earnestly. "I know. In the old days"—Ralph's parents winced at this—"the kids who played it were considered nerds and losers. But now those nerds are running movie studios or starring in billion-dollar comic book adaptations." He leaned forward. "My dad loved it and got me and my older brothers hooked. When I came to Brooklyn, I found out there are all sorts of people my age who are into it."

"Are you saying you still play it?" Ralph's dad asked incredulously.

"Sure," Declan said. "Who wouldn't want to be a barbarian raider for a few hours a week, battling orcs or dragons instead of your cell phone company?"

Declan turned to Ralph. "What do you think, Ralphie boy?"

Declan always had nicknames for Ralph. This one came from some old TV show called *The Honeymooners,* which Declan swore was the funniest thing ever but Ralph just thought was dumb when he watched a few episodes on YouTube.

Ralph didn't have to think. He'd just finished reading the Lord of the Rings trilogy for the third time. This sounded really awesome.

So it was settled. Declan would lead a game of Reign of Dragons for the kids. His role, it turned out, was to be the game master, or GM, as it was called. He would narrate a story, which he came up with especially for Ralph's party. Ralph was fascinated by this. He'd never heard of a game where there were no set rules or goals. This was open-ended.

Declan turned to Ralph and said, "If you want, we can pick another RPG. Reign of Dragons isn't the only one. There are tons of them."

"RPG?" said Ralph.

"Yeah, you know, role-playing games. . . . Hey . . . wait a minute. . . ." Declan's eyes narrowed. This was a bad sign, Ralph knew. He could sense another nickname coming.

"What's your middle name, again?"

"You know what it is," Ralph said. His mom, like moms from time immemorial, always used his full name when she was mad at him. ("Ralph Peter Ginzberg! Did you leave the top off the ketchup bottle again?")

"Peter, right?" said Declan. "So your initials are RPG? That is so epic. It's the same as—"

"I know," muttered Ralph. He had a feeling this one was going to be around for a while.

3

THE FELLOWSHIP OF THE RPG

Ralph assumed that when Declan showed up for the party, he'd bring a board and some game pieces. Instead, as he unpacked his knapsack, Ralph—or RPG, as Declan almost always called him now—was intrigued to see a stack of books, pads of paper, pencils, and sheets of paper with all sorts of charts on them. There was a board of some kind, but it was more like a grid. And lots of funny-shaped dice.

Noel's eyes lit up at the sight of the books piled next to Declan. He devoured anything having to do with fantasy, and as soon as he'd heard about the party, he'd bought the player's guide to Reign of Dragons. Ralph could tell from the expression on his face that Noel already considered himself an expert in the game.

Declan began to explain the rules: "So here's how this works. Before we even start to play, you all—"

"—have to create our characters! I've already done mine!" Noel broke in enthusiastically.

"That's not fair!" Jojo said, jumping up from her seat. "He's got an advantage!" She looked like she was about to punch Noel. It wouldn't have been the first time.

Declan didn't even flinch. He nodded appreciatively. "Noel, it's really great that you've done some work beforehand, but let's all start from scratch together. You cool with that?"

Declan turned to Jojo. "It's totally cool, Jojo. This is a whole different type of game. You're not competing with each other, you're working together as a team."

"Wait. There's no winner? What kind of game is that?" Jojo groused.

"Trust me, you'll see," said Declan.

"Can you have a character that sings?" asked Persephone, of course.

Declan nodded. "It depends on the story and the characters you're playing," he said.

"That's FANTASTIC!" yelled Persephone, jumping up and down.

It turned out the sheets in front of them were for helping to create the characters they would play. There were all sorts of choices, and everything was up to them.

First they got to choose their race, meaning they could be an elf, a human, a dwarf, or a halfling, which was a little like a hobbit.

Okay, a lot like a hobbit.

Pretty much exactly like a hobbit.

But the man who created the game, Warwick Wycroft, didn't have the rights to use the word *hobbit*, Declan explained. So halfling it was.

And then they chose their character's class, which meant

its job—whether it was a fighter, a wizard, a rogue, or something else. Declan explained that a good group had one of each class, to balance out the strengths and weaknesses of the other characters. They all could be fighters, but then they might get into a situation where they needed a rogue's cunning or a wizard's spell, and then they'd be in a bind.

To no one's surprise, Cammi immediately chose to be a mysterious elf wizard, and Jojo promptly took the role of a powerful kick-butt barbarian fighter. Persephone was thrilled to learn there was a character class called a bard, who basically cast spells by singing.

But Ralph thought it was a little funny that Noel chose to play as a cunning, sly halfling rogue. This didn't seem like Noel at all. Rogues were masters of bluffing, cheating whenever possible, and lying when it served them. Noel, on the other hand, seemed compelled to tell anyone and everyone exactly what he thought.

For example, he might say, "Wow! I don't mean to be rude, but that's one ugly sweater!" But he'd say it so good-naturedly that it was hard to be too mad at him. He was just saying what he felt.

The only one left was Ralph.

"So what's it gonna be, RPG?" Declan asked as he wrote down the other choices.

Ralph had been thinking the whole time. Who was he? He wasn't really a fighter like Jojo, and he wasn't good at keeping secrets the way Cammi was. He certainly wasn't going to be another bard. And he couldn't see himself as a rogue.

He looked down at the player's guide he had borrowed from Declan's pile. "So what does a cleric do, anyway?"

"Well, the cleric is kind of misunderstood," Declan began. "He's sometimes seen as a supporting role, healing the other members of the team or protecting them or granting them more powers, because he can't cast as many battle spells as a wizard. But in some groups, he or she can be seen as the leader. He protects his group and makes decisions that can be the difference for his comrades in encounters with evil forces between life and death."

"Okay . . . ," Ralph answered, "I guess I'll play the cleric."

"Good man, RPG," said Declan. "You know, I'm a cleric in the game I play with my friends. A dwarf cleric."

"Yeah, I think that's what I'll be too," said Ralph. And they high-fived.

As Ralph rushed to fill out his sheet with statistics for his dwarf cleric, Declan turned to the others, a mysterious smile creeping over his face. He picked up a twenty-sided die.

The dice controlled everything: whether they would be surprised or would surprise their enemy, the order in which they could attack, the amount of damage they would take or mete out—all was decided by rolling one of the dice. There were six: one four-sided, one six-sided, two eight-sided, one twelve-sided, and one twenty-sided. Declan referred to them with the letter *d* and how many sides it had, as in "Roll a d4 to determine your skill at deceit."

"All right, my fellow adventurers," he began, opening his notes. "Let the adventure begin!"

MEETING THE PRINCE

During that first adventure, the group had found themselves in the tavern of the Gray Rabbit, where they encountered a mysterious cloaked man who had told them of a quest.

"We are in a battle for the very soul of our world," Declan had said, in the creaky voice of an old man. "I need adventurers for a quest that will bring them glory and untold riches if they succeed."

He turned to Persephone. "What do you want to do?"

Persephone looked at the others. "Can we trust this guy?"

"He seems suspicious. You should challenge him to a fight!" Jojo said eagerly.

Noel looked up from his copy of *The Reign of Dragons Monster's Guide*. When it wasn't his turn, he was poring through it. "Maybe he's a demon from another world. It says here there are creatures called Demiurges who can shape-shift and—"

"I think we should leave and look for a room somewhere else," Cammi said. "It sounds risky, and we're not powerful yet."

Ralph was silent. Persephone nudged him. "What do you think, RPG?" They had all started calling him that, and he kind of liked it.

"I think you should roll for a perception check," he said. "Maybe you can see if he's honest."

Persephone nodded and rolled the d20. "Eighteen!" she squealed. "Yay!"

Declan grinned. "That's a great roll. Look at his hand and see that he wears a ring that bears the crest of the Morgorath. He must be of the Royal Family."

Declan turned to Cammi. "What do you do now?"

Cammi said, "We kneel at his feet and say, 'We await your orders.'"

Declan nodded. He consulted his notes. "The man pulls back his cloak, revealing that he is indeed Prince Andromodus, ruler of Morgorath. He tells you that in order to foil the plans of the evil Duke Cormorant, the prince must regain the Serpent Scepter."

Ralph looked at the others. "Does Cormorant know about the scepter?"

"Yes. He searches for it as well. The last of the ancient wizards who created it divided the scepter into seven pieces, after foreseeing the rise of Cormorant. Each piece was sent off on one of seven ships, each going to one of the seven islands that neighbor Demos."

Five anxious faces leaned forward.

"But the pieces must be found in the correct order," Declan continued. "If you just collect the pieces at random, you will break the spell. But the clever wizard left a puzzle to be solved. Find the answer to that puzzle and it will lead you to the first island."

"So?" demanded Noel. "What's the first puzzle?"

Just then the doorbell rang. There was a flurry of noise upstairs, with footsteps and loud voices.

"Welp, looks like we have to end there. Your parents are here, and—"

There was a chorus of "No fair!" "This stinks!" "Come ON!" The three hours had flown by.

Persephone's mother appeared at the door. "Sweetie, it's time to go."

Declan was collecting his dice, rolling up the board, and putting the pencils and pads away. "It's all right, Persephone. We have to stop now anyway."

"We can't stop there!" protested Ralph. "It was just getting good! We don't even know the first puzzle!"

Jojo crossed her arms. "I'm not leaving until you tell us."

Declan looked at the kids and shot his fingers through his hair. "Well, we could continue the game next week. Let me talk to your parents. . . ."

And just like that, the weekly RoD group was formed.

IN THE GREAT HALL OF ANDROMODUS

"Please step forward," the herald declared.

"Well, my new friends," said Bram, "it looks like we have moved up in the world!" Gerontius nodded. He was the quietest back at the tavern, but the wizard held himself like a leader, and somehow they all seemed to regard him as such.

Mirak gazed around the vast throne room of Andromodus. Heavy velvet tapestries hung from the ceiling, obscuring the windows. All the light came from the huge chandeliers, each festooned with what looked like hundreds of candles. The furniture was made of warm, dark wood, matching enormous columns, each of which featured one of the seven ancient mages, the wise ones who had made the Seven Serpent Scepter, carved in relief.

As they walked forward and approached the throne, Jandia instinctively grasped the hilt of her broadsword. She trusted few, and was not about to let down her guard because of some fancy talk and finery. But if there was an adventure to pursue, she was willing to listen.

The young man who bounded out of his seat and ran to greet them was quite different from when they had met him at the Gray Rabbit. Gone were the rags and tatters, which had been replaced with robes of fine silk of dark ruby red. Jandia also wore red—a bright blood-red cape symbolizing all the Kreel who had perished at her blade.

"Welcome, my champions!" exclaimed the prince as he warmly shook their hands. "Let us make haste, as the scoundrel Cormorant is still gathering his forces."

He led them to a broad oak table covered with scrolls and parchment. He unrolled one and spread it out before them.

"The only clue we have," declared the prince, "is somewhere on this map."

On the scroll was a map of the whole of Demos, including the islands on which each piece of the Seven Serpent Scepter was to be found, if the tale was true.

Gerontius pointed to an island near the port city of Breukelyn.

"The first will be found there," he said with a nod.

The others leaned in. Torgrim stroked his beard. "It looks like all the others."

"How can you see that so quickly?" asked the astonished Andromodus.

"Elves see things that others do not," Mirak said, smiling. "Do you have a tool to see closer?"

The prince clapped his hands, and a large magnifying glass was brought to him, encased in brass. He held it over the island the wizard had indicated.

Now it was clear. He shook his head in amazement. In the smallest possible hand, so tiny that it was almost hidden by the letters identifying the island as Fahrenthold, someone had drawn a green snake.

The prince's eyes lit up. "Amazing! But I expected nothing less from you!"

He turned to the group. "I shall have a boat in the harbor prepared. You sail at dawn!"

The quest had begun.

A SERPENT UNCHAINED

By the flickering torchlight, all could see the two reptilian kobolds lying dead at Jandia's feet.

They had arrived on Fahrenthold Island only a few hours earlier to explore the now-deserted coastal city.

Torgrim peered up at the jutting cliffs that surrounded the port like massive hands held up to ward off whatever evil still haunted the place since its abandonment after the Great Wars. "A fitting place for an ambush."

Gerontius motioned toward a brace of columns that were crumbling into ruin, like the rest of the structures that dotted the main street. "Our search leads there."

Bram led the way. He held out his hand and pointed downward. There, beneath what appeared to be high grass, were metal plates, rusted but possibly still deadly.

Torgrim nodded and reached to pick up one of the heavy pieces of masonry that littered the street. Bram scampered back to the others, and the dwarf grunted as he heaved the stone onto one of the metal plates. Immediately, the plate gave way with a groan, and sharpened steel rods shot up from the ground surrounding it.

The group gathered around the plate, and Bram carefully pulled it up, revealing a set of stairs twisting down into darkness. A dusty torch was attached to the side wall a few steps down.

Mirak nocked an arrow into her bow, and Jandia took her broadsword from its sheath.

Gerontius stepped forward and whispered into his glowing orb, which sent out a shower of beams and lit the torch. Bram carefully took the light from its holder and began his descent, followed by the others. As he reached the bottom stair, he immediately recoiled. The others could see the tear in his sleeve and blood staining the fabric. Torgrim rushed forward, grabbed Bram's arm, and began muttering a healing spell. The bleeding stopped. "What was that?"

Bram turned to answer, when suddenly his eyes widened, and he pulled the dwarf down, just as an arrow whistled by his ear.

There was a *thunk* as the missile found its mark and a high-pitched groan as a kobold fell dead at his feet.

"The demon was my target," Mirak said calmly. "There was no need for such theatrics."

They stepped over the body of the small, vicious creature in his crude armor.

Jandia moved to the front. Two other helmeted kobolds were playing some sort of dice game at a rough-hewn table. They were arguing, which was why they hadn't heard their comrade fall. They turned at the sound of her approach, but with one stroke she slew them both.

She peered into the torchlight. This was an old dungeon, with chains attached to the walls with stout rings. Some of the chains still held the skeletal remains of ancient prisoners who had had the misfortune to come before them.

It was Gerontius who spotted it. A small smile played across his lips as he walked over to a section of wall that looked at first glance like any other. "See how this one differs from his brothers?" he remarked, pulling at a chain attached not to circular ring, but rather to a square bracket. The bracket pulled away from the wall, revealing a hidden compartment. He lifted his hand to reach inside, when Bram called out.

"For such a wise and powerful wizard, you would not be so foolish as to put your hand where it might be chopped off," he said.

Gerontius nodded but looked annoyed. "I am grateful for your counsel, Rogue, but I am capable of making such decisions myself."

Bram shrugged. "As Your Most Majestic Highness wishes. I will refrain next time and we will see if our friend the dwarf has the ability to reattach hands or other necessary body parts."

Jandia leaned down. "Listen, *friend* rogue. You will speak in a nicer tone or I will sever more than our friendship."

"Yes, yes," said the rogue. "Understood." Bram joined the wizard by the small hole in the wall and peered in. He took the torch from the wall and shoved it in. He pulled it out and examined it. He sniffed the air. "No poison gases released. No traps unleashed." Bram turned to Gerontius and bowed low. "Good wizard sir, you may proceed."

Gerontius gently nudged Bram out of the way and reached in. He rubbed caked dirt from a small object in his hand and wiped it on his robe to show the others.

It was a small statue of a crawling snake, made of iron.

Torgrim held his torch up to the bricks next to the hole. "There is something painted here."

It was faint, but hard to miss. A lizard and a bird.

Since Ralph's birthday was in late April, six weeks had flown by before it was time for summer vacation. They had found the first serpent, and no one wanted to stop.

But both Persephone and Jojo were going away to sleep-away camp, and Cammi was visiting his father and stepmother in California. Noel was off to Grenada to spend months with his grandparents and cousins on his mother's side, which he found way more fun than his dad's stuffy old New England family. It was agreed they'd pick up in the fall.

Ralph was the only one staying put. Other than a week visiting family in Chicago (where he tried in vain to get his cousins interested in RoD), Ralph's mom and dad had too many projects lined up for them to take time off. So he spent his summer immersed in books about RoD. He was amazed at how many there were. Even a whole fantasy series based on someone's campaign! As summer ended, he was more eager than ever to return to their adventure.

DEEPER INTO THE WORLD THEY GO

Fifth grade was even better. Once September rolled around, the group began meeting again.

Ralph wasn't the only one obsessed with the game. All five talked about it endlessly at school, and after school as well, with discussions both in person and online, trying to decipher the latest puzzle or determine the best course of action to defeat the newest enemy. And always the insidious forces of Cormorant seemed to draw ever nearer. But they had yet to find the elusive second serpent. The months passed, as different theories were tried.

Persephone had suggested that the second clue could mean an island that had both birds and lizards, and Noel had thought maybe if they could find out what species of lizard and bird the pictures showed, it might narrow it down a bit.

It was Ralph who finally realized they were to put the two pictures together.

"A flying lizard!" Cammi agreed.

"Which means a dragon!" added Jojo.

It made sense that Ralph would be the one to figure it out. Of all of them, he was by far the most dedicated. He had collected all the books for birthday and Chanukah presents, and he had even purchased miniature figurines of each of the adventurers (called "minis" by veteran RoD gamers) to place on the game mat in order to keep track of their movements. He and Noel spent most afternoons sitting in one or the other's room quizzing each other about stuff like the number of hit points that were needed to defeat a certain sea monster. By asking around at the various shops and taverns back in Breukelyn, they learned that dragons were extinct, for the most part. There were rumors about one island, though, but some chalked it up to legend and fairy tales. But it was worth a trip to find out. Declan put the minis on the board and rolled the d20.

Then the story took a shocking turn:

THE DRAGON GIRL

It was not big, as dragons go, but it was a dragon nonetheless. Standing about as tall as a good-size elephant, it was a brilliant cerulean blue, and it was dying.

When the party arrived on Draakland Island, they had hoped to find evidence that dragons had lived here long ago. They wanted to find the next serpent piece and move on, but there the dragon was, big as life and flapping its wings. Then they noticed the arrows deep in its flank. The shafts were striped, markings that showed they came from Kreel bows.

It circled pitifully above them, gasping, as small jets of smoke escaped its snout.

Exhausted, the dragon finally landed with a giant thud upon the sandy beach, writhing and moaning. Jandia was about to put the poor creature out of its misery with one death blow when Bram cried, "Wait a bit!"

Jandia, not used to being addressed so forcefully by the halfling, turned in surprise.

Gerontius stared down at the creature. "Bram Quickfoot is right to call out to you. See, the dragon is changing its form."

And so it was. The dying dragon's scales were being shaken off, vanishing in little puffs of flame, like bits of paper escaping from a bonfire. What was left was assuming human form.

It was a young girl, of a sort. Her jet-black hair was matted, and she was breathing with great difficulty. She was robed in the same blue as the dragon's scales, which was stained with her blood. She lay quietly for a moment. Then she raised her head.

Jandia pulled back her sword arm, sensing danger. But the girl's sad eyes caught hers, and Jandia lowered it.

Finally, the young girl spoke barely above a whisper. "You are sent by Andromodus, like the others, I presume?"

Gerontius shook his head to the others. "We seek the serpent but serve no master," he said carefully.

The dragon girl coughed, and laughed. "I know the truth, Wizard. I have eyes. They are dimming, but they see still. He has bid you find the serpents before Cormorant attacks his castle."

Torgrim leaned in. "You are in need of healing. Perhaps I can help."

"I am beyond help," the girl said in a simple voice. "I only stay here in this plane for one purpose."

"And that is what?" asked Jandia.

"To give you a warning. Andromodus is not who you think. He is not the rightful heir to the throne. The Serpent Scepter will grant him power to rule all of Demos with the strength of a thousand armies."

This speech seemed to take much out of the youth, who closed her eyes and rested for a moment.

"This is quite an accusation to throw at one who is not here to defend himself," said Gerontius.

"Use your spellbook, Wizard. Seek the truth."

Gerontius murmured an incantation and gazed into his orb. His expression was grave as he turned to the others. "The orb of wisdom confirms that what the dragon says is true."

"But what of Cormorant? He does not raise an army?" asked Torgrim.

"There is no army. Cormorant is of the Blue Order, sworn to protect the serpents at all costs."

"How do you know this?" demanded Bram.

With her dying breath, the girl raised her head. She stared fixedly at them. "Have you not guessed? I am Cormorant, fifth of that name, keeper of the silver serpent!"

The youth was fading fast. "I beg you. You can see I have no army. I charge you with the task of finding the rest of the serpents. Go as you were, but do not bring them to Andromodus. It is for you to protect the scepter until its rightful owner finds you."

Her head fell forward and she was no more.

The group stood still, letting her words sink in as a wind whipped around them.

As the young girl died, her robe had fallen open at the throat. Bram's keen eye spied it first. It was a silver serpent charm, hanging from a slender silver chain. He reached around and gently removed the second serpent.

"There is something in the serpent's mouth," he announced to the others.

He held it up, and Mirak peered at it closely. "It appears to be a tiny parchment scroll."

Bram's small, nimble fingers carefully unrolled the paper. It was blank. He handed it to the cleric with a shrug.

Torgrim studied it for a moment, then reached down and blotted the parchment on some of the blood from the dragon girl's tunic. As soon as the blood touched the paper, two more images appeared. A crown and a mouse.

"Pah! More riddles!" muttered Jandia.

No one had seen THAT coming!

Well, Noel insisted that he had known Andromodus was bad all along, but the others knew he was just talking.

As the game had progressed, Declan informed them when they had gone up a level, and with each level up they would be granted more powers and spells. Of course, this also meant the monsters and enemies were more powerful as well.

Declan had a magical way of keeping the story moving forward, injecting a new NPC—or nonplaying character, as all the various innkeepers, guards, knights, and assorted allies and enemies were called—just when things began to feel predictable. Finding the third serpent proved harder than the first two. It seemed that no one in the port towns knew which island would match the picture.

And it was not safe to venture back to Athanos, knowing now that Andromodus was using them for his own ends.

To keep things interesting, Declan prodded them to add more background to their characters, giving the histories and experiences, which were reflected in how each had come to the group.

Noel, of course, had five pages of notes on his character. "It was three hundred years ago when the first Quickfoot rogue, Patrack, was famed for his use of cards to cheat travelers at his inn, the Ratfaced Wanderer—"

"Um, it's great you have his whole family tree there," Declan said gently, "but maybe we can skip ahead to where it's about Bram."

Noel shrugged. "That's cool. I can put the rest up on the website I created for our campaign so everyone can read it there. It's really interesting."

"I think I'd rather eat my own boogers," suggested Jojo.

"You do already," Noel answered.

"I do not!" Jojo growled, and balled her hand into a fist.

"Whoa. Settle down," said Declan. "Let's just talk about our characters, okay?"

"Bram Quickfoot was orphaned at birth, his parents having been slain by the infamous lizard-man Orak-Thule." Here Noel held up his copy of the *Monster's Guide* and showed a picture of a scaly-headed bad guy. "Bram was taken in by a wandering group of thieves, pickpockets, and bandits who adopted him and taught him their ways. By the age of twelve, he could pick any lock, cross any threshold undetected, and disable any sentry with a silent strike of his daggers, Salt and Pepper, before they could raise the alarm."

Declan high-fived Noel. "That's great work, Noel. Who's next?"

Jojo leapt up. She had scribbled a few things on a sheet of loose-leaf paper. "Jandia Ravenhelm is the last of her tribe, a fierce warrior race of humans. The men stayed at home and the women fought the battles and did all the cool stuff. One fateful day, a Kreel war party wiped out all the men while the women were out on a hunting party. They returned to find their homes burned. The stench of burning flesh made them sick, while the pools of blood—"

"That's fantastic," Declan interjected. "Very, um, evocative."

"I haven't gotten to the good part," Jojo said, "where they find the pile of—"

"We get it, Jojo," said Persephone, who looked a little pale. "Could you maybe not be so yucky?"

Jojo made a face. "Whatever. I was just trying to set the scene."

"And you did great," Declan said. "So what happened when they found the . . . mess?"

"The women made a pact to return to their village only after every Kreel had been removed from the world. One by one, the best Kreel assassins had hunted them down, until Jandia, feared by all of the Kreel nation, was the last one left."

Jojo sat down and smiled and nodded.

Declan turned to Cammi. "You're up."

Cammi sighed and took a tiny square out of his pocket. He unfolded it carefully, and Ralph could see it was covered in tiny handwriting.

Cammi cleared his throat. "Ummm . . . Gerontius Darksbane is descended from one of the oldest and most respected noble families of wizards, going back to the earliest days of elven history. He was being groomed to take over the duties of his father, the high wizard of the FaerieField Wood People. But something occurred that was a terrible and tragic secret. This betrayal earned him banishment forever."

He stopped and refolded his paper.

"That's it?" asked Noel. "What was it?"

"It's a secret," said Cammi, tight-lipped. "I can't tell you."

Declan nodded. "Secrets are cool. I hope it shows up in the story somewhere."

"Maybe . . . ," Cammi said slowly, looking like it probably wouldn't.

"My turn!" Persephone yelped. She stood up, throwing her papers on the table and walking into the center of the room.

"You forgot your notes," said Ralph, holding them out.

Persephone shot him a look. "I've memorized them." She took a deep breath, closed her eyes, and began. "Poor misunderstood Mirak Melodin. As a half orc, half human, she was accepted in neither race. She was the product of—"

"An orc warrior having taken a human woman as his war bride," Noel cut in. He turned to the others. "I read all about half orcs in the player's guide."

Persephone glared at him. "No, she wasn't."

"But that's how half orcs are made!" protested Noel.

"Not in my story," Persephone said. "Mirak was actually the product of a great forbidden love between an orc maiden and a human prince. Their passion was so great they went against the traditions and laws of both their races."

"That's so romantic," murmured Cammi.

Persephone raised her hands to her forehead. "Rejected by both the orcs and the humans, the baby Mirak was left on the banks of a river, where the water people, the mermen and mermaids, took pity on the poor creature and raised her."

At this point in the telling, Persephone was so overcome with emotion she began to weep.

"We can go on to Ralph," suggested Declan.

Persephone held up her hand. "I can continue. This poor child, born of love that was not accepted but was pure as any in the realm, was given a gift by the gods: a voice of such great beauty that the merpeople chose to train her from birth to be a bard, teaching her the songs of the great sirens of old and the powerful ballads of the ancients, giving her powers that she herself scarcely knew. On her sixteenth birthday, they gave her a glorious harp, bejeweled with gems taken from the vast treasure of the ships wrecked at the bottom of the ocean."

There was a pause as she finished. Then they all applauded, and she bowed.

All eyes turned to Ralph.

Ralph could feel his armpits getting wet. How could he possibly top that? He looked at his notes. Next to the stories his friends had told, his dwarf cleric looked completely ordinary.

"Let's see . . . ," Ralph tried. "Torgrim was a priest of his religion who had committed some, um, heresy against his god and was banished."

"Wow, what a coincidence," Noel said. "Cammi's character was also banished already."

"That's okay," Declan said quickly. "I'm sure Ralph's story is different."

"It is!" Ralph added quickly. "In Torgrim's case, he had fallen in love with a high priestess."

Persephone rolled her eyes. "I did the forbidden love thing already, RPG."

Now Ralph was getting mad. "Let me finish! She didn't love him back, so it's different, okay? So he prayed to their god to bring harm unto Gundulf, the one she desired. Such a selfish and destructive prayer backfired on Torgrim. Instead of harming the rival, it brought a terrible fate unto Torgrim himself, scarring his soul so that every dwarf woman who would ever look upon him would do so with disgust. His shame was so great, and the mark of guilt so terrible, that he left his order, to return only once he could prove to his god through his selfless acts that he was worthy of having the curse removed."

That did the trick. Persephone had started to cry again, which he had to admit wasn't all that big a deal.

These three hours each Saturday were the highlight of Ralph's week. What did it matter that he had gotten a bloody nose in kickball or that Cecille Hayes had laughed out loud at him when he mispronounced "epitome" in English vocabulary? (Who knew it was pronounced "eh-*pit*-uh-me"? Well, Cecille did, apparently.) Each Saturday he would assume the role of the great cleric, and with the other adventurers (who by this time were well-known throughout Demos) defeat evil and search for the remaining serpents of the scepter.

8

THE KNOT UNTIES

The last session of the year before summer vacation was coming to a close, and Declan didn't seem to be his usual amazing self.

He had brought the group to what seemed to be an uninhabited island, but instead of filling their heads with details and bringing it to life as only he could, he barely sketched the details and was content to let the kids come up with the rest.

At the sound of their parents arriving upstairs, Ralph waited for Declan to clap his hands and say, "We shall meet again in the fall!" like he did last year, but instead he cleared his throat and looked down at the floor.

"Okay, I have some news for you."

"Is it bad news?" Cammi asked.

"No, it's good news, at least for me," said Declan quickly, then adding, "but it kind of changes things. . . ."

"Changes things how?" asked Jojo, her body tensing like Jandia ready for battle.

Declan began to pace the room. "You kids . . . you know how I love to tell stories, right?" he began. They nodded and he continued. "And I've gotten as much out of these sessions as you have. But I don't just make up stories for you. I also like to write stories for myself. That's what I'm hoping to do for a long time."

"Cool!" said Noel. "Like fantasy stories for kids? You'd be perfect! We'd read them for sure."

"Actually, I've been kind of writing for grown-ups. About grown-up things."

"Hey, that's totally fine," said Ralph. "I bet your stories are great."

Declan ran his fingers through his hair. "They're not great. I mean, not yet. I need help learning how to make them better. So I'm going back to school to do just that."

Persephone laughed. "School? But you graduated already! Why are you going back?"

"To get a graduate degree," Declan said, leaning forward. "I've been accepted to one of the best creative writing programs in the country."

"That's amazing!" said Cammi.

"So that's why you were so distracted today?" Noel said.

"Well, there's a little more news," said Declan. "Because, you see . . . the program is in Iowa."

Persephone backed away in horror. "That means . . ."

Ralph glumly finished her thought. ". . . you'll be moving away and won't be able to run our game anymore."

The others fell into a stony silence.

Declan looked around helplessly. "It's okay. It'll be okay."

"How?" wailed Persephone. "It's ruined. It's over."

Jojo shook her head. "Enough, Persephone." She looked at Declan suspiciously. "How is it going to be okay? You were the one running the game."

"Maybe Declan knows some other person who can come in and run it from here," suggested Ralph.

"I do know a few guys who could GM for you," Declan said.

"But it won't be the same," grumbled Cammi, crossing his arms. "They won't know all our histories, all the things that have happened—"

"I would give them my notes, but it's true that no one knows this campaign the way I do," Declan said. He then cast his eyes around the room. "And the way you guys do."

Noel brightened. "Do you mean one of us could be the game master? 'Cause I've been practicing at home, and I'd love to do it!"

This set Persephone off on another crying jag; Jojo looked like she wanted to punch someone, anyone; Cammi just lay back looking at the ceiling; and Ralph groaned.

"I didn't mean just one of you should do it," Declan explained. "I meant more that it could alternate. Each one of you brings something different to the story. I bet it would be amazing too."

Ralph made a face. "Yeah, but . . . it's your story. You're the one who made it up."

Declan looked sheepish. He pulled up the screen that separated his dice and sheets from the players. There was a laptop there as well. "Not completely. If you go online, you'll see that there are campaigns that have been played by other players and put up on this site called GMstories.com."

There were dozens of entries on the page, with statistics showing how often the various stories had been downloaded.

There was the Rose Queen, the Shadow of Morgorath, the Butterfly Sword. But at the top of the list was the Seven Serpent Scepter.

"The SSS is one of the oldest campaigns ever waged. It was written by the creator of the game himself, Warwick Wycroft. Literally thousands of RoD'ers have played it through the years. Of course, it's different each time, depending on the characters the players create and the story that they help to tell. But the puzzles are all in there. All you have to do is follow the basic text and bring your own imaginations into it and it will be incredible. Like it always has been."

Declan powered down his laptop and gathered up his things.

Ralph asked a question, even though he knew the answer already. "Is this our last session with you?"

Declan kept his back to them. "Yes, it looks like it. I didn't want to say anything until I knew for sure, or I would have told you sooner—"

To no one's surprise, the end of his sentence was cut off with Persephone's mournful wail. Jojo glared at him. "I know it's for the best and everything, but this totally stinks," she growled. But she gave him a grudging hug as well.

He turned, and it was clear that his eyes were wet. He rubbed them and sighed. "Yo, RPG! You have my email. Keep in touch and let me know how the game is going. You know I love you guys."

And just like that, he was gone.

Ralph's mom poked her head into the room. She surveyed the somber and depressed scene. "I guess Declan told you, huh?"

Ralph stared at her. "You knew?"

"He made your dad and me promise not to tell. He didn't want anything to get in the way of the game."

"This is actually pretty neat," Noel called. He had pulled up the website on Ralph's laptop. "Maybe we could do this."

"I guess it's worth a try," Ralph said grimly.

9

WHO GETS TO TELL THE STORY?

There were lots of changes that fall. Sixth grade meant more homework, and now that Declan had gone, Ralph's big sister Gabrielle (who everyone called GG) was put in charge of hanging out with the kids on Saturday. She wasn't happy about it, but it meant babysitting money, and all she had to do was sit in her room, where she could study, watch videos, or text her friends.

At lunchtime at school, the group met to discuss exactly how the game would proceed. They had agreed that to make it fair, the GM was to read only far enough ahead to see what happened during his or her own GM session. Ralph had brought his d20, and suggested they roll it to determine the order of who would GM. Noel got the highest roll, followed by Jojo, Cammi, and Persephone. Ralph ended up in the last slot. He decided that wasn't all bad. He could learn from the others' mistakes.

Noel arrived at their first session, his eyes glowing. "I've been working all week on this," he said, opening his notes and unfolding the game mat. He had marked it up with a new island, and he plunked their minis on the water just offshore. . . .

THE REALM OF RATTUS

Gerontius was studying the map as the boat approached the island of Kendzion. "Are you sure this is the right island?"

Mirak, who had been strumming upon her harp and singing, paused. "Do you question my sisters?"

It was Gerontius who had suggested that she call upon the merfolk who had raised her. Surely they would know if an island had mice and a crown. The last full moon she went out onto the foredeck and called out to them, and three mermaids swam alongside the ship, laughing and calling back. They sang one word to her: *Kendzion*.

"I hope we reach land soon," Bram said. "This trip is growing tiresome."

Torgrim pulled at his oar and gritted his teeth. Since the boat had been lowered off the side of their ship, he had done the lion's share of rowing. Bram was idling at the prow, his fingers dangling lazily in the water. Torgrim glanced at him. "Halfling, I seem to recall that each of us was to take a turn at the oars."

Jandia, who was also hard at work, nodded. "We have all labored at this. It is your place now."

"We each have our job to do," answered Bram. "Mirak, to sing songs that ease the burden; Gerontius, to interpret the signs and portents hidden in the charts and maps; and I, to use my keen eye to scan the horizon."

"Perhaps, Rogue, it would profit you better to keep your keen eye on your surroundings," said Mirak, nocking an arrow in her bow and letting it fly.

There was a nasty squeaking sound as the missile found its mark. Bram looked down to see a giant rat turn belly up next to the boat, and beyond it, dozens more. He quickly pulled his hand up, his face pale. "True words, Bard! We are besieged!"

The water was fouled with the greasy fur of the huge, nasty creatures, each the size of a small dog. They swiftly brought the oars in and drew their swords.

It was quick work, but the frenzy of the combat was such that the band had not realized how close to the island they had come until their skiff ran aground with a loud crunching noise.

Torgrim was busy with the chore of healing everyone's bites and scratches, and so got the worst of it, tumbling into Jandia, who in turn knocked Mirak over.

Only Bram had noticed that they were not alone. On the shore was a greeting party: hundreds of rats dressed in armor. They were surrounded. Jandia managed to bring her sword down on one of the rat soldiers, but the blow glanced off, leaving no mark.

"How is this so?" she asked. "This blade has cut through the skin of the toughest dragons and elf-made armor!"

Mirak gaped in astonishment to see her arrow miss a target at point-blank range, veering off to the side before it could strike its target. "This island is bewitched!"

Gerontius peered into his orb with a worried expression. "I fear my powers seem to have been diminished as well."

Quickly, they were overrun and disarmed. The filthy creatures dragged them inland to a crude structure, a castle of some sort. Inside was a throne room, and perched on the throne, sitting over them, was an awful sight.

He was a three-headed rat, glorious in his grossness, wearing a silk blouse made for a man, his giant furred belly poking out between the buttons.

There was a crown on each of the heads, and all three regarded them with equal contempt and scorn. The clue of the mouse and the crown clearly led here.

One of the soldiers who brought them kicked Jandia in the back. "Kneel before King Rattus and show homage."

Jandia whirled to face her tormenter, but Gerontius touched her arm. "We are outnumbered and need answers. For now, we should do as ordered."

They all lowered themselves, and the middle head of the king spoke. "Ah, good to see that new guests have arrived. It has become so boring since the last party."

He clapped his massive paws. "No time like the present. What shall we do with these?"

A small rat, dressed in what were probably the stolen clothes of some unhappy warrior who had come before them, cocked his head. "Make them fight against one another. To the death, Your Highness."

Rattus yawned. "We have done that far too often. I crave something new."

Bram's sharp ears heard a familiar noise, which filled him with some small hope. It was the sound of dice being shaken in a cup. There, across the room, was a pair of soldiers, gambling.

"Majesty," Bram asked, gesturing toward the two. "May I inquire what they are doing?"

Rattus gave the soldiers a bored look. "A stupid game. They play at dice, wagering over which will get that lovely bow after the half orc meets her death, I warrant."

Mirak instinctively reached for her weapon, then remembered they had been disarmed when they'd been captured. She lowered her head.

"There are ways to make the game more interesting," Bram suggested.

All three of Rattus's heads yawned. "Bah. That is a game for fools and children."

"Ah, but what makes it a game for kings is the stakes," countered Bram.

The pink eyes of the rat king focused on the halfling. He looked intrigued.

"And what," he hissed, "do you propose? I already have your lives."

"We each roll once. He who rolls the higher number is the victor. If I win, we go free, as do all who are imprisoned here, by magic or other means."

Two of Rattus's heads laughed. The third regarded his captive with interest. "And if you lose?"

"We forfeit our souls," the halfling said simply.

There was a gasp from his party.

"You must not do this!" said Torgrim, clutching his amulet.

"I will never renounce my soul, to my last breath," declared Jandia.

Bram calmly looked at the king. "How do you answer, Rat King?"

Rattus's three heads laughed, each in its own way. One was a deep rumble, another more of a hee-haw, and the third a high-pitched titter. It was most unpleasant. "For one roll of the dice? In my own kingdom, where your magic is useless? I agree to these rules!"

Mirak grabbed Bram's sleeve. "This is reckless and mad."

Bram pulled his arm away and turned to the others with a small smile. "Trust me."

Torgrim looked downcast. "All my life there have been two truths above all others: never eat the fish at the Crusty Bucket in Athanos, and never trust a halfling rogue."

Jandia turned to Gerontius. "Speak, Wizard."

Gerontius's face was impassive. "We have no choice," he said simply.

The hideous king clapped his paws and gestured for the two soldiers to bring the dice and the cup forward.

"No, Majesty, not those dice," said Bram, reaching into his boot. "We play with mine."

Rattus bared his teeth. "What nonsense is this?"

"We made no rule as to whose dice would be used," said Bram, rolling the large twenty-sided die in his hand. "Or is the Great King Rattus afraid of being bested by a halfling rogue in this simple child's game?"

A murmur went through the court. The king looked about.

"We play with your little trinket," the king muttered. "Little difference it will make to you. I am the only magic here."

Bram bowed. "I offer to let the sovereign of these lands take the first roll."

Rattus took the die from Bram's hand in his paw. Six sets of eyes examined it, until all three heads were satisfied it was not specially weighted in any way. "Very well, see if you can beat this." He shook the die in his paws, closing his eyes as he did. "There!" he cried, and let it tumble onto the floor between them.

Nineteen. A cheer went up from the court. That would be hard to beat.

Bram took up the die and rubbed it on his shirt. Only Gerontius's keen eye noticed the switching of the die. He looked at the others and winked. "We shall win the day yet," he said.

He kissed the die and said, "Lady Luck, she who watches over all rogues, cutpurses, and thieves, smile upon me this day!"

He dropped the die on the floor, where it spun like a top on one of its edges. As it twirled, not a breath could be heard in the vast court.

Then it dropped.

Twenty.

A scream of agony ripped through the air. The king rose, clawing at his fur. He seemed to be in a fevered frenzy to be rid of his very skin. The dreadful smell of sulfur and brimstone filled the room, and a cloud of acrid smoke billowed from the throne. The adventurers doubled over, coughing. There were screams and shrieks from all over the court, as if something terrible was attacking the other rats of the court.

But as the smoke cleared, it was apparent that rather than being attacked, they were being released. The shades of demons large and small floated downward, back into the underworld from which they'd come. In their place they left humans—the rat forms were gone. Where the hideous king had loomed now sat a man with a dark red beard. He was clothed in a striking purple robe covered in golden stars. Upon his head was a velvet conical hat. He was a wizard.

Gerontius knelt before him. "Ragus, my old teacher! How amazing to find you here!"

Ragus smiled. "Rise, Gerontius. It is I who should kneel to you. Or to your small friend, who lifted the curse that has kept us captive these many years."

He beckoned to Bram. "Come forward, my brave little rogue. And take your reward." Ragus held out his wand. "I meddled in things that no wizard should. I lost not only myself to the demon Immodius, but all of my court as well. For freeing us from this life of misery, and to ensure I will not be tempted again, I give you my wand."

"You cannot!" Gerontius exclaimed. "A wizard's wand is—"

"I must," Ragus insisted. "Please, take it and go."

Bram regarded the item in his hand. It was of the finest crystal and made in the shape of a serpent.

"The third serpent!" Bram explained. "But where is the clue that is meant to come with it?"

"There is something I was told," Ragus said, "when I was given this wand. But it was a long time ago. . . ."

"Do try and remember," Torgrim muttered. "It would be extremely helpful to us."

Ragus rubbed his temples and thought for a moment. "It is something to do with the sailor and his song. That is all I can recall. Forgive me."

10

OKAY, MAYBE NOT NOEL

"That does it," Jojo said, pushing Noel off his chair and grabbing the pages from the campaign he had printed out.

"What are you doing!" screeched Noel. "I'm the game master! You can't look at those!"

Jojo surveyed the pages calmly. "I can and I will. Look, guys, there's nothing here that says our characters lose their powers. You made that up so your character would be the hero."

"I was just trying to make the game more interesting!" protested Noel.

"That's not what Declan would have done," Cammi said. "He would have found a way for all of us to figure it out together and gain our powers back."

Noel picked up the rest of the papers and threw them at Jojo. "Fine. It's your turn to be the GM. Everybody obviously thinks I'm doing a sucky job." His lip was trembling.

Ralph looked at his friends. He'd never seen them like this

before. "Guys, we all need to take a step back and chill. It's just a game."

Noel laughed. "That's funny coming from you, RPG. You keep saying it's the greatest thing that's ever happened to you."

"I have to admit, Noel's right," Jojo said. "That's why you're probably the best person to run the game."

"You are really into it," Persephone added. "I mean, not that the rest us of aren't, but . . ."

They all nodded.

"Look, we agreed we'd go in order," insisted Ralph. "That's what Declan would want us to do. Follow the dice."

Jojo shrugged. "If that's how you feel, I guess I could give it a try next session."

THE BATTLE FOR THE SERPENTS

The five adventurers sat at the table, each lost in their own thoughts. It had been a struggle from the moment they'd landed at the grimy port city of BlackBriar.

First there were the bandits at the dockside, who had fallen upon them, attacking from all sides. Torgrim had been able to throw up a protective shield, which had given them just enough time to draw their weapons. Jandia handily dispatched three of the brigands with a single stroke of her sword, while Bram used Salt and Pepper to finish off the remaining two.

Then they proceeded toward the Ghoul's Maw, the name of the tavern given to them by an old beggar as a natural meeting place of old sailors.

Following his directions, they found themselves at the

mouth of a pitch-dark alley. Gerontius used his orb to bring light, which revealed giant spiders gliding toward them, mouths open, ready to strike.

It was harder to fight off the spiders than the bandits, but Mirak's arrows were true, and she dispatched the queen, who landed on her back, squashing a number of her children, sending black blood spraying everywhere.

And finally, as soon as they arrived at the tavern, the stench of suspicion rose from every table. The barkeep, a grubby, muscled half orc, leered at Mirak as she walked in. She ignored him.

Jandia had had enough of this town. In an instant, she pulled him over the bar and smashed several nearby bottles of grog over his head. He staggered, and the rest of the room went silent.

The barkeep shook his head to clear it and stared at the party in front of him. Then he laughed, spit some blood onto the floor, and shuffled back behind the bar. "Five pints, on the house."

And that was only the beginning of the adventure. They all wondered what challenges this fourth serpent would bring.

From the corner, an ancient toothless man wheezed away at an antique sailor's hornpipe:

> *"The Isle of Zwaardwood Has a Tree of Swords*
> *Raise the sail and up she rises!*
> *It's taken the lives of Knights and Lords*
> *Raise the Sail, boys, we're bound away!"*

The adventurers exchanged glances.
"Then it's the Isle of Zwaardwood, is it?" asked Bram.

"Or just a drunken sailor spouting nonsense," grumbled Torgrim.

"Well! Are these the fabled Serpent hunters all of Demos speaks of?" asked a voice.

They turned as one to see a tall elf clad in black leather from head to toe. Although as slim and elegant as Gerontius, he could not have been more different. He had a nasty smile, and was expertly twirling a small sword in his gloved left hand.

"Who is it who asks?" said Torgrim wearily.

"I was not addressing you, Dwarf Ugly," said the rogue elf. "I can barely stand to look at you."

Torgrim gripped his hammer but did not take the bait.

"Ah, but I am being rude," said the elf. "Please, let me introduce myself and my party. I am Gandaril, and this is Markon," he said, indicating a human wizard clad in armor at a nearby table.

"And may I present Grokk, Brimblebeard, and Faffnung," Gandaril continued, pointing to a brawny orc fighter hefting a heavy oaken shield; a small, nasty-looking goblin who seemed to be a druid; and a dwarf ranger armed with a pitted and battle-worn ax.

"Well met," Bram said, his hands on the hilts of his daggers. If there was to be a fight, he would be ready.

"Well met indeed," laughed Gandaril darkly. "We have been searching for you."

Jandia had had enough. She kicked the table over, drawing her blade. "Enough! If it is a fight you wish for, have at it!"

11

JOJO LOSES THE BATTLE

Jojo looked up from her notes, the d20 in her hand.

Persephone was looking out the window, Noel was reading a book, and Ralph and Cammi looked bored out of their skulls.

"What?" she demanded. "Is there a problem? I thought this was going great."

Cammi spoke up timidly. "It's just that . . . well, it seems like all we're doing is fighting."

Jojo tossed her papers so they flew everywhere. "You think this is easy?"

"I'm sorry! Forget it!" Cammi said, pulling down the bill of his baseball cap to escape.

Jojo threw the die onto the board with such force it bounced off and rolled under the couch. "Sor-reee. I was trying to make it more, you know, fun."

Ralph sensed this was only going to escalate, and he felt that some healing was in order. He was a cleric, after all. "You were doing a great job," he lied. "And I'm sure it's hard to come up with something we all can get into."

Jojo regarded him for a second. Then, grudgingly, she handed the notes to Cammi. "Here. Next week it's your turn. Good luck. You think I did such a bad job."

"I didn't say that!" moaned Cammi. "I just thought—"

"I know!" said Jojo. "I'm sorry. I didn't really like being the GM anyway. You're the one who always comes up with such great stories."

They all had to admit this was true. Besides the plays he came up with at home, whenever there was a writing assignment in class, Cammi's were always the most imaginative.

Cammi looked at the sheets in a panic. "So, RPG . . . how does this work, anyway?"

Ralph looked over his shoulder. "These are notes . . . suggestions to get you to the next serpent. The best way to do it is to cover up all but the paragraph you're using. That way you don't know where the story is going."

Cammi looked skeptical. "So I can make up the rest?"

"With our help," Ralph added quickly. "You know, like with Declan."

Cammi nodded, and a small smile appeared on his face. "Sure. This could be really fun. . . ."

THE ELF'S KISS

"Master Cleric," Bram gasped as he slapped at his arm for what felt like the hundredth time, "are you sure you have no healing spell for biting insects?"

Jandia was up ahead, slashing at the dense undergrowth of the junglelike forest they had found on the Isle of Zwaardwood. No villages, no taverns, not so much as a hut. Just jungle. And no tree of swords to be found.

Mirak closed her eyes and strummed her harp. She began to sing a song that connected her to the birds and creatures around them. She was asking for guidance.

Gerontius raised his head. Elves were usually at home in woodlands, but this strange place, with its heavy, perfumed air, made him uneasy. All around him were flowers he had seen nowhere else in all his travels.

Mirak opened her eyes and smiled. "They tell me that what we seek lies no more than fifty paces ahead."

"Can you ask the birds to eat these blasted bloodsuckers?" griped Torgrim, waving his hand in front of his face as Bram nodded vigorously in agreement.

Mirak looked amused. Somehow she was untouched. "I did. You should no longer be troubled."

They finally reached a clearing. The air changed as they broke through the jungle, bringing a welcome coolness to their flesh and presenting them with an extraordinary sight. A huge tree, tall and broad, stood before them. Branches reached out on all sides, and the trunk seemed to rise into the clouds. High above them, a canopy of leaves blocked out the sun. All around the tree, fernlike plants with long, sharp leaves stuck up from the ground like a natural fence.

As the party approached the tree, they were surprised to hear someone call out, "Hold! Come no farther!"

The figure was impossible to see at first, clothed as it was all in green. A hood covered its face, and it was perched on one of the lower branches.

Bram called, "Good day! We mean you no harm!"

"Good day to you. Please leave me in peace. I wish no harm to befall you as well, but it will if you stay here," the figure responded.

Mirak took a step closer to get a better look. The figure turned toward her. "You were warned. Will you never listen? You all seek the same thing, and I am left to watch you fail."

Gerontius peered at the figure. "Show yourself, dear one. I sense you are of my people."

The figure shyly lowered its hood and was revealed to indeed be a young elf, with long blond hair and icy blue eyes. He looked at Gerontius. "You are exceedingly lovely and fair of face, as pale as the snows of Nivis." He said this as if he were stating a fact, like "The sky is blue."

"How do you know of the snows of Nivis?" asked Torgrim.

"The others who have come before you have spoken of it. So many others . . . ," the elfling murmured.

"I am Gerontius Darksbane, of the FaerieField woodland people," the wizard said.

"They will mourn your passing," said the elf boy as he turned away.

"Where are you from?" asked Mirak.

"Where indeed?" The elf smiled.

Jandia grunted and raised her sword. "Enough riddles."

Gerontius raised his hand to stay her, and took a step closer. "Have you been enchanted? Has someone put you on this island?"

The boy looked the wizard full in the face. "I came here by choice, and I believe I will never leave."

"We can help you," Torgrim said. "I am a healer, a cleric of the Orach'T'char."

"I need no healing," the boy said simply. "And I beg you once again, come no farther, on pain of death."

Jandia squared her shoulders. "I see nothing to fear. I feel you wish to keep us from reaching that which we desire."

She stepped forward.

There was a shaking from the ground, and before their eyes, the ferns surrounding the tree rose from the earth, changing, becoming arms, each with a sword attached. They waved about in arcs, hundreds of them. There were swords of all kinds, from giant broadswords to curved blades from faraway lands. They created an impenetrable barrier between the youth and the adventurers.

"So this is the Tree of Swords?" asked Bram. "What enchantment have you done?"

"I have done nothing!" the boy replied. "The tree protects itself. These are all that is left of the scores of seekers who have come before you. As they fall to the tree's weapons, they join the rest in her protection."

Gerontius looked in his spellbook, turning the pages furiously.

Torgrim approached him. "Surely there is something that can be used to thwart this cursed demon tree."

The wizard shook his head. "It is a deep magic. I am not familiar with it."

Mirak touched his arm. "Perhaps there is a way that is not found in books."

Gerontius thought for a moment, then nodded. He turned to the boy. "You feel you have a secret no one knows. You are different."

The swords slowed. The boy sat still, regarding the wizard. "You can see this?"

"You think the sharp swords that imprison you are from the tree."

"I know they are," insisted the youth.

"And I know they are not," said the wizard. "Many of us have trees like this of our own. They are of our own creation. Your fear has made the swords. In your soul, you feel they protect you."

"What you say may be true, but I need them!" the boy cried out.

"You do not wish to escape this tree?"

"With all my heart," said the boy grimly. "But it cannot be."

"It is in your power to do so," said Gerontius as he stepped forward.

"Come no closer!" the boy begged. "I have no wish for you to die!"

"I shall not die," Gerontius said simply. "You will not let me."

The wizard stepped directly into the path of the whirling blades, his arms raised.

Mirak screamed and hid her face.

A giant arm pulled back a mighty battle-ax. It arced through the sky.

"We see you as you are, and that you are good," the wizard said.

The blade passed through him harmlessly, fading away with the others.

The meadow under the giant tree was quiet, save for the sobbing of the young boy. He crumpled and fell from the tree.

Gerontius ran to him and scooped him up. He then looked around and called to the others.

"There! In the branches! There is something glowing!"

They joined him at the bottom of the tree. High above, they could clearly see a glowing branch.

Bram nodded. "I can climb."

Jandia peered up. From the branch where the boy had sat, all the way to the higher reaches, where the glowing prize awaited them, there were no branches. "That may well be, but there is no purchase."

Mirak pulled four arrows from her quiver. "'Tis a good thing you are so light, Halfling. Perhaps I can create a ladder where there is none."

"Excellent thought, good bard!" exclaimed Bram. "If you would start at that spot where the knot is?" He indicated a place high above them.

The arrows found their marks, going deep into the tree, leaving enough for the nimble rogue to reach the desired branch.

Jandia shook her head. "You can climb branches, and you can climb arrows, but the first foothold is too far away. How do you propose to reach it?"

"This is not something I thought I would ever say to you," said Bram, bowing to her, "but would you hurl me up there?"

Jandia laughed and bowed back. "How often I have wished to do this! And now I can do it to further our cause, instead of simply to stop your tongue."

She grabbed him as if he were a child and hoisted him to her shoulder.

Torgrim closed his eyes and said a prayer to help her aim.

With a grunt, she hurled the halfling up. He stretched, and with a lunge grabbed on to the first arrow. It held.

"We make a great team, eh?" he called down.

"Save your breath and get the blasted branch!" Torgrim yelled back.

As Bram carefully made his way up the tree, Gerontius was gazing at the boy in his arms.

The boy looked up at him. "I am Samiel," he said, and smiled.

"Welcome to the world, young Master Samiel," said Gerontius, and leaned down to kiss him on both cheeks, the traditional elvish greeting.

"I do not think I can leave this place yet," said Samiel.

"You will leave it when you are ready," replied the older elf. "Some of us leave our forests when we are young; others must wait until they know themselves better."

Samiel nodded. There was a shout from the branches. Bram could be seen carefully edging his way along the large branch underneath the one that glowed. Tentatively he reached out and grabbed it with a cry of triumph.

As he did so, the branch under his feet gave way and he hurtled toward the ground.

Gerontius turned, and with a sharp gesture, the air around the halfling seemed to grow heavy and slow his fall. He began to drift downward, finally landing in Jandia's surprised arms.

"Why, my barbarian beauty, I had no idea of your feelings for me!" Bram laughed. "And see what I have—Ow!"

Jandia had dropped him on the ground. Bram rubbed his backside with one hand and held out his prize with the other.

It was no ordinary branch. It was the handle of a scepter, fashioned out of wood in the shape of a serpent.

"But what of our clue?" asked Torgrim.

Mirak regarded Gerontius. "I seem to recall the comparison young Samiel made of our wizard friend's pale complexion."

12

PERSEPHONE'S REWRITE

When Cammi had finished, the reaction was mixed. Persephone and Jojo thought it was incredible.

Noel? Less so. "Yeah, I guess the tree stuff was cool, but that kissing stuff was kinda mushy."

"I'm sorry. I shouldn't have put that in," said Cammi, pulling down his baseball cap and slumping down onto the floor.

"Don't listen to him. He is a loser," pronounced Persephone, fixing Noel with a killing look.

Cammi sighed. "No, he's right. I should have had more fighting, like Jojo."

Ralph hated this part, where someone seemed to always need to put down the other's attempt. "That's silly, Cammi. You did great. It was . . . very you."

"Yeah, that's for sure," said Noel. "It had you all over it."

Jojo smacked Noel on the arm. "He's just jealous because you're a better game master."

"He wishes," muttered Noel.

Ralph was glad he didn't have to follow Cammi. He handed the dice ceremoniously to Persephone, who looked like she'd won an award or something.

Persephone let him off the hook. "I promise that next week will be a story no one will ever forget."

Cammi laid his head on her shoulder. "I can't wait."

THE BARD AND THE MINSTREL

Had there ever been a world without snow? The climb had been so long, wading through drifts that came up to the half-ling's thighs, that try as he might, Bram could not remember what it was like to see sunshine and clear skies. Was it only yesterday that they had arrived on Nivis, sent here by the words spoken by Samiel of Gerontius's snowy white face?

"Curse that elfling! I'd rather break my neck than perish out here in some frozen waste," Bram muttered. The wind howled so loudly, he could have screamed it, and no one would have heard.

Mirak had been trying to keep up their spirits by singing "Ninety-Nine Bottles of Grog on the Wall."

"By the gods, I have had enough of this song," Jandia bellowed over the winds that whirled about them. "If you do not cease, I shall hurl myself off this accursed mountain."

"Would you prefer 'If Thou Art Happy and Thou Know It, Clap Thy Hands'?" Mirak asked. "We can sing that instead."

"I would prefer to have my ears cut off with a dull ax, to be honest," answered Jandia in a very rude voice.

Gerontius could be heard faintly ahead of them, calling

them forward. Looking behind and noticing the halfling struggling so, Jandia sighed and tugged him out of the snow and carried him under her arm like a sack of flour bought at market.

The wizard held his orb up, and the beam shone weakly into the densely falling whiteness. A short ways ahead of them, a light seemed to flicker. Torgrim nodded eagerly and set the pace, his stubby but strong legs churning the snow around them as he ran as best he could, his beard caked with frost.

The flickering had come from the mouth of a cave set into the mountain. With numbed hands, Jandia lowered Bram and pulled her great sword from its sheath. There was no telling who or what was in that cave, but there was fire and fire was warm, and that was enough to risk even a cave troll or a garrison of goblin warriors.

Bram slid ahead of her. He was after all, the smallest and quietest and had the instincts to smell out traps before the rest. He peered in and then gestured to the others to proceed with caution.

They entered the cave and the sudden quiet of the large open area came as a shock. The whistling winds continued outside unabated, but here only the crackling of a large fire could be heard.

It took a moment to get used to the relative darkness of their surroundings, having spent so long in the unending whiteness of the mountain. But they were soon aware that they were not alone.

Stirring a pot over the fire was a curiously dressed figure. "Please join me and be welcome," he said in a voice both deep and melodious.

He was dressed in striped silk hose, with a checkered doublet with long puffed sleeves gathered at the wrists. His hair was pomaded and combed back, and his elegant mustache was waxed and curled up at the ends. Upon his head was a purple velvet cap, with a large peacock feather attached to it. He made an altogether ridiculous picture but seemed harmless.

The party moved warily toward him, and he ladled some of the stew into a bowl and held it out in front of him. "You are cold and in need of food, I warrant. There is enough for all."

Torgrim eyed the bowl hungrily. He moved forward. "Good sir, we have interrupted your meal. Please eat first, and then we will join you."

The man paused to reflect on this and then burst out in a deep, easy laugh. "Oh, I see. You fear I have put something in the soup. I admire your prudence. I have eaten already, but if it eases your cares, then by all means." He raised the bowl to his lips and drank a large sip. He swallowed it down. "You see? It may need some salt, but otherwise you should find it agreeable."

As they ate, Gerontius studied the man. "You have not honored us with your name or story. Who are you, who has saved us in this storm?"

The man smiled, took off his cap, and bowed. It was a courtier's bow, with many gestures and much hand-waving. "I am Chioni, official court minstrel to Andromodus of Athanos."

Jandia tensed and reached for her sword, but Gerontius gently waved her down. "I take it, Minstrel, that you are aware of who we are."

"But of course," said Chioni, crossing his arms. "All Demos sings your praises."

Bram threw the remains of his bowl into the fire, which flared up. "Does that include Andromodus?"

"As a matter of fact, he is exceedingly disappointed in your decision not to bring him the fruits of your labor," the minstrel replied, "and has sent me to ask you to see reason."

"Reason has nothing to do with it," said Gerontius, "but rather who is the rightful owner of the scepter."

Chioni looked concerned. "Ah. So it is like that. Well, suppose I put this to you more in the way of a challenge. You seek the fifth serpent. I have found it."

Mirak regarded the minstrel. There was little love lost between minstrels and bards. The former thought bards used their songs for war and magic, instead of for the beauty of the song itself. Bards found minstrels little more than simpering court servants, playing at the pleasure of their duke or prince, singing insipid songs of praise for unworthy patrons who paid them handsomely for their meager talents. "How did you get here?" she asked suspiciously.

"Do not think that Andromodus has no magic of his own to call upon," said Chioni. "He has been able to follow your journey on his Map of Enchantment, which shows not only you, but also all the others he has sent on the same quest."

"He knows we are here?" demanded Torgrim.

"Of course. He has sent me by a spell of transport before you to take what is rightfully his."

Jandia's eyes were slits. "Brave words, when you are one and we are five."

"You kill me, and you will never find the fifth serpent."

"And we are to hand over the others to you, just like that?" Bram asked, laughing.

"Not at all," the minstrel replied. "I propose a simple contest. If you win, you get the serpent I have found. If you lose, I leave with yours."

His face betraying nothing, Gerontius stared calmly at the man. "What type of contest is this to be?"

Chioni smiled broadly. "A simple one. A singing contest, between the bard and myself."

"What nonsense!" Bram said. "Whoever heard of such a thing? And who will be the judge?"

"I will challenge you to armed combat," Jandia said, "which will be easy to judge, as you will end up in a puddle of blood."

"It is a song contest," the minstrel said. "And the judgment shall be rendered by the four Great Winds—North, South, East, and West—who bless those of us with the gift of singing."

Gerontius raised an eyebrow. "And how will we know their verdict?"

"They will make their decision known," Chioni replied, "when they stop their wailing and sit silent."

He turned to Mirak. "Are you in agreement?"

Mirak slowly picked up her harp and tuned it. The weather had loosened the strings, and it was now warmed by the fire. "I do not feel music is a thing to be judged. All who sing are blessed, from the commonest shepherd to the finest fool who sings for his supper in the court."

Chioni sighed. "That is a shame. In that case, your quest ends here, as only I have the fifth serpent."

"I will sing, but only for the Winds, who have blessed me with my voice and who play sweeter music than any mortal," Mirak said, and sat cross-legged near the front of the cave.

Chioni the minstrel joined her with his lute. "Shall I go first?"

"As you wish," she said softly.

Chioni cleared his throat and began:

"The snow fills the valley.
My love waits for me,
but I am lost.
I cry out, but my voice is taken
by the winds, and none can hear.
O, Amortas, Goddess of the North Wind,
Send my song to her.
Alas, that she will see me nevermore!"

The minstrel's voice was deep and sweet, seductive and sad.

It was Mirak's turn. She raised her chin to the skies, plucked her harp, and began:

"Ye winds of the North
Will head back to your home.
Your children await you
To sing them to sleep.
The tiny breezes, the yawning zephyrs,
The gales and the gusts . . ."

Mirak's voice was not as sweet as Chioni's, but it was clear, and rang like purest crystal.

Chioni sang a second verse of a sailor lost at sea, crying out to Syandra, goddess of the South Winds.

The whipping winds seemed to be dying down. What had been a gale was now gusts.

"The Winds are listening," Torgrim muttered to Gerontius, who nodded.

Mirak sang a second verse of her song, as the mischievous little winds of the South were set in their beds by their mother.

Chioni's verse sang of a farmer, crying out to Evandra, she of the East Winds, to bring him breezes so that his crops' seeds would scatter and reward him with heavy wagons of food come the harvest.

Mirak sang of Evandra soothing her little waterspout, who was crying. She rocked him in her arms.

There was yet a breeze in the air. Neither had caused the winds to cease.

Chioni closed his eyes and sang his last verse.

> *"My lover fills my heart,*
> *The buds do burst so in spring,*
> *But I am lost.*
> *May you, Wysteria, Goddess of the Western Winds*
> *Send my song to her,*
> *And like the Snowbound, the Sailor, and the Tiller*
> *I will sing of the greatness of the Four Winds evermore!"*

There was total silence as the chord from the minstrel's lute echoed in the cavern. There did not seem to be even a breath of wind.

With a look of triumph, Chioni bowed low and turned to Mirak. "The Winds have listened and made their choice."

Mirak hung her head and wept. Great tears splashed upon the surface of the stones of the cave.

"Wait!" Bram cried, and pointed at Chioni's cap. The peacock feather fluttered. It was hard to see, but there was the gentlest of winds, kissing the feather. There was a whisper, from far away, but all could hear: "We have not chosen. We await the last verse."

Mirak looked up and plucked her harp once more.

> *"Hear me, O Winds,*
> *Who lullaby your little ones*
> *To their cloud beds,*
> *My voice is not as pretty, and my verses may not be as*
> *smart,*
> *But the minstrel's pretty words come from his pretty head,*
> *While I, your humble servant, sing from the heart."*

The peacock feather grew limp and lay against the side of the fine velvet cap. The winds were still. There was a parting of the clouds, and the sun shone.

Gerontius spoke. "The winds have made their final call. Will you dispute it, Minstrel?"

Chioni calmly took off his lute and held it out in front of him. He slowly walked to the fire and put it in.

Mirak gasped. "Your lute! No!"

"It must be done," the minstrel said as he watched the flames lick the veneer of the priceless instrument.

They gathered around the fire, watching as the lute burned, faster and faster, the flames leaping up and disappearing into the darkness above.

Finally, Chioni reached into the ashes and pulled some-thing charred from the fire.

"It was hidden inside the neck of my lute."

He knelt before Mirak and gave it to her. It was a flute, made of bone. As the others looked on, it began to twist in her hands, until it rested there, in the form of a serpent.

Carved into the bone near the mouthpiece was a finely wrought sea scene, of a boat being drawn down into a swirl-ing tower of water.

"Is this a clue or a prophecy?" asked Jandia.

"Perhaps both," answered Bram. For once, he was not smiling.

13

RPG IS CHOSEN

Jojo threw herself on her back and began to snore.

"Enough singing!" said Noel finally. "I vote one song at most per session."

Three other players held up their hands.

"Anyway, that was totally not how it goes in the story," Noel continued. "They just go into the cavern and find the bone serpent in the rib cage of a kobold skeleton."

"I was trying to make it more interesting!" Persephone said, pouting.

"More interesting for you, maybe." Jojo smirked.

Ralph narrowed his eyes. "Wait a minute. Noel, how did you know what was going to happen?"

"I read ahead," Noel said casually.

Persephone was livid. "No fair! We all promised not to do that!"

"She's right," Ralph said. "Why would you do that?"

Noel shrugged. "Because I wanted to."

Not unexpectedly, Persephone burst into tears. "I was so selfish!" she sobbed. "I have been acting unforgivably! I am a terrible, awful game master!" She ran from the room.

"That was acting?" asked Noel.

Persephone bounded back in the room and walked up to Ralph as if nothing had happened. She presented him with the notes and the dice.

"Your turn, RPG," she declared.

Ralph looked down at the board.

It felt right. He felt a jolt of excitement go through him. He could bring together everything he had learned from all the books, and all the countless sessions watching Declan balance the various personalities around the table, and keep the action going. He was ready.

The next Saturday, Ralph began as GM.

All had to agree: the game changed as soon as he stepped in. It was decided that he would be the GM from now on.

From the moment in January when he took over, Fridays now became Ralph's second-favorite day of the week. That was when he would begin to plan in earnest the journey he would take his friends on come Saturday, trying to find ways to help them move their characters forward.

For inspiration, he would often venture online. Warwick Wycroft had long ago sold the game to a large company, which had created an entire industry of ancillary goodies, including small figures you could place on the map during the game to match your character, and fictional books about brave heroes' and heroines' adventures in the fantasy world. Fans throughout the decades had also written their own stories and posted them online for all to read. And there were countless forums where players could compare strategies for making the game the best it could be, or just complain about members of their groups.

Ralph had made friends online with a number of older GMs (he had been careful not to tell them too much about himself—he had learned in school when they showed that video with the corny name "Don't Get Caught in the Inter-NET!"). He had originally gone on to ask for advice about how and where to get the final serpent to complete the campaign. The adventure he was following was tantalizingly vague about this.

He learned that this was one of the great mysteries of the RoD world. The Seven Serpent Scepter was the last campaign actually written by the Great Wycroft before he sold the company, and he had deliberately left it unfinished. It was up to each GM to try to defeat the ultimate, seemingly unstoppable, monster.

Ralph had been chronicling his group's journey and discovery on the forum dedicated to the search for the Seven Serpent Scepter. There were many comments when he reported that their fifth serpent was the bone flute and not simply a bone taken from the kobold. Some congratulated him for bringing something new to an old campaign (he was always careful to credit one of his players for coming up with this), while others complained that part of the challenge was following the rules as set down in the adventure.

The game was a welcome distraction from the real world— right about the time he had become game master, Ralph had gotten braces. Sixth grade was hard enough without a mouthful of metal to contend with.

As spring approached, there was something even more distressing creeping into the game. Ralph was starting to suspect that the game simply wasn't as important to his friends as it once was.

As hard as he worked to keep the game as exciting as possible, he had to face the truth.

Although Jojo was still wearing sweatpants and keeping her hair pulled back in her regulation tight ponytail during the weekend games, she had begun to wear it down at school. Now she wasn't just doing gymnastics camp in the summer; she had also made the school team.

All of a sudden, she had started dressing more like her teammates. She was spending more time with them, too, no longer eating lunch with the RoD group. That was okay, because she seemed to enjoy her time with her old friends during the game. But once the fights over who was going to be GM started, it felt like RoD was mattering less and less to her.

And Noel, who once would sit and discuss strategy with him for hours, was moving into computer games. He had found some online game about rocket ships and exploring other planets that it seemed like half the boys in the sixth-grade class were playing.

Ralph had tried it, but it didn't do anything for him. Not that he didn't enjoy playing at his friends' houses on a gaming console or playing on his PC. It just wasn't as special. Everyone played *Space Adventure,* but the RoD campaign was theirs. They had made it together, creating characters and a story no one else ever had. And each of them had worked so hard and experienced so much together.

Then Persephone was cast as the lead in the middle school

play, to no one's surprise. It made total sense that she would start to hang out with her theater friends, but Ralph was a little hurt that Cammi had joined them, too, once he had volunteered to work in the costume shop, sewing the dresses and other clothing.

Cammi did seem happier than Ralph remembered ever seeing him. And Ralph's parents told him when he had complained about this at dinner one night, "Ralph [they were the only ones who still called him that, apart from his teachers], part of being in sixth grade is finding your tribe. Your group. The kids you want to hang with. You have to allow Cammi and the others to do that."

The only thing was that Ralph thought he *had* found his tribe. They all had seemed as into the game as he was. And now they were deserting him.

14

THE QUEST TO END ALL QUESTS

It hadn't helped that the search for the sixth serpent was the most annoying, and this was about the time Ralph could feel the group starting to get restless. The picture on the bone was a waterspout, which turned out to be the name of a port city on the Isle of Nyfitsa. For some reason Wycroft set it in a small bustling town instead of some mystical castle or deserted ruin. It seemed so ordinary when the pompous Lord Mayor of Waterspout proudly gave them a tour of the various buildings, ending at town hall, where in his office they spotted in a glass cabinet behind the mayor's desk a jade serpent. Inquiring after it, they were told it was a relic from the founder of the town, and its most prized possession. Of course the rogue tried to steal it and was promptly thrown into jail. The wizard tried to enchant the Lord Mayor into giving it to them but rolled too low a number and instead ended up turning the mayor's pet cat into a tortoise.

Ralph had learned from his online GM friends that this was some sort of test of the GM's ability. There was a theory that Wycroft had deliberately made this quest as endless as he could, so that the few teams that managed to stay with the adventure this far would be unlikely to want to continue. The forum was rife with stories of groups voting to move on to another adventure because this one had become ridiculous. It was as if Wycroft had wanted only the most determined players to finish his campaign.

The adventurers were given the task to perform a series of challenges in order to free Bram and attain the jade serpent. These were tedious chores, like collecting all twelve overdue books from various citizens for the town library (Wycroft clearly had a sense of humor), and demanding ones, like figuring out how to untie the untieable knot that had kept the great sailing ship of the town in port.

Somehow, Ralph had kept them going until the final task, when Persephone realized that the Lord Mayor was actually an imposter, a goblin who had created this town in order to trap them here and get from them the other parts of the great scepter for himself.

In unmasking him, she had broken the spell, and the town disappeared, along with the false Lord Mayor, leaving only the jade serpent behind. Since one last island remained, it was clear where they needed to go.

But the damage had been done. What enthusiasm was left felt like it was waning with each passing week.

Even when Ralph brought them the incredible news he'd learned from the website.

RoDCon was coming to Brooklyn. The yearly gathering

of Reign of Dragons lovers. People dressed as their favorite players, and there were round-the-clock games as well as celebrity appearances (it seemed that some of the biggest actors and directors had played the game when they were young and still had fond memories of it). There was a picture of a man with a lean face and a ponytail, and under it was the announcement that Andy Wycroft, the son of the game's creator, would be there.

None of which impressed his friends. Apparently they all had something better to do that Sunday. Ralph decided he didn't care. He would go alone if he had to. Sure, the tickets were expensive, but it was going to be a birthday present.

And it had finally arrived, the weekend after they had found themselves on Valtti Island, deep beneath the mountain Morgorath among the ancient stones of the Temple of Kamach'Ldar. With the Kreel army having been decimated, only the deadly Komach'Kreel was left to defeat before finally collecting the last serpent.

What the others didn't know was that this was the most powerful monster in all of the campaigns—practically impossible to defeat, even for characters at levels as high as their own.

Every hit from the Komach'Kreel dealt an incredible 200 damage, and even the most powerful healing spell from a cleric couldn't counter that. It was as if Wycroft was daring his players to come up with a solution to an unsolvable riddle.

Ralph had scoured the forums and message boards for clues to how to defeat the Komach'Kreel, but other than by cheating, it seemed that no one had ever gotten past this point in the game.

Which was why the location of the seventh scepter was never mentioned. Wycroft had simply written, "Those who have beaten the Komach'Kreel will find the answer within themselves, and the game will end with the heroes bathed in glory and remembered for generations to come."

15

OONA AND LUNA

After the last Saturday, when Jojo seemed ready to quit, it should have come as no surprise to Ralph that when he passed her locker between classes, she stopped him. "I need to talk to you."

"Sure, what's up?"

Before she could answer, Jojo's scowl was replaced with a huge smile. Ralph didn't need to look behind him to know what had happened. Oona and Luna, two of Jojo's teammates from gymnastics, had arrived. They pushed past him like he didn't exist (which he probably didn't, in their minds) and surrounded Jojo. There were squeals and hugs as if the girls hadn't seen each other for months instead of since the day before.

Oona and Luna wore identical warm-up jackets, and Ralph noticed all three had matching friendship bracelets. They also all wore the same shade of eye shadow. It wasn't Ralph who noticed this; Cammi had pointed it out to him during one of the few lunches they had had together. Cammi was amazing about seeing things like that with girls. But then again, he spent so much time with them. He was more clued in to that kind of thing.

"Jeez, could Coach Stephens have been more irritating yesterday?" said Oona or Luna. They talked so fast and finished one another's sentences, so it was often hard to tell who was saying what.

"I know, right?" Jojo said, sounding very un-Jojo-like. "What was with that running like a thousand laps? I needed to work on my vault."

"Your vault is awesome," said Oona/Luna. "You rock so hard!"

Jojo tossed her hair and looked up at the ceiling. "Gah. I wish. I just sometimes feel like, you know, you guys are so supportive I don't know what I'd do without you."

The girls hugged again. As they continued to ignore him, Ralph amused himself by deciding that he had cast a spell of invisibility. This lasted until Noel passed by.

"Hey, RPG, you going to history?"

"I'll be right there," Ralph answered. "I think Jojo wants to talk to me about something."

Oona and Luna seemed to notice him for the first time. "Oh. Were you guys talking or something?"

Jojo looked horrified. "Um, I was just asking . . . Ralph . . . about a problem on the math test."

Oona and Luna exchanged glances. "Well, he should know about that."

All three burst into giggles. Ralph tried to figure out what was so funny. He assumed it meant he was clueless about everything else.

"You sure it wasn't about some magic spell or something?" Oona or Luna asked.

Jojo's face took on a look of disgust. "He wishes."

More helpless giggles. "We'll let you guys talk—we have to get to chorus." And they rushed off, leaving a trail of some flowery-smelling perfume in their wake.

Ralph was trying his best not to show his annoyance. He didn't want to get Jojo mad. He'd seen her mad plenty of times during the game, and it wasn't pretty. "Third period is going to start in like two minutes. What did you want to ask me?"

Jojo looked into her locker, slowly picking out the books she needed for the next few classes. It seemed she was deliberately not looking at him as she spoke. "Listen, I'm not sure I want to, you know . . . do the thing anymore."

Ralph knew where this was going, but he decided to make Jojo spell it out. "Um, sorry, Jojo, could you be more vague? 'Cause I have no idea what you're talking about."

"You know. The Saturday thing."

Now it was Ralph's turn to get mad. "You mean our campaign? You won't even say the words *Reign of Dragons* at school now? It's that embarrassing to you?"

"You really want me to say it?" Jojo asked. Ralph should have known better than to provoke Jandia Ravenhelm. Unlike Cammi, she wasn't afraid of confrontation. "Okay. It's not that it's embarrassing, Ralph. It's just . . . you know, it was fun for a while, but I have a lot of other priorities now. Gymnastics takes up a lot of time, and there's homework and—"

"And texting or Instagramming with Oona and Luna and Gaga and Goo-Goo, or whatever their names are." Ralph snapped. He wasn't sure if he was madder at her no longer calling him RPG or her suggesting that she was suddenly too cool for a game she'd loved for so long.

"So what? Since when is what I choose to do with my time your business? Have a great time with the others. You can kill off my character or something."

"First off," Ralph said evenly, "I don't know how much longer Persephone and Cammi are going to want to play either, and second, I think it's really sad that you can't even call Jandia by her name. You'd just kill her like that?"

Jojo turned to him. "She's not a real person! Gah! I am so over all of this!"

Ralph realized he was going about this wrong. He had to strategize. This was a battle, and he was facing a much more powerful opponent. He needed a weapon stronger than hers.

Jojo turned to go.

Ralph stopped her. "Please. Jojo. I promise you next week we're going to find the seventh serpent. It's the end of the campaign we started two years ago. Don't you think you owe it to the others to at least see this through to the end? If you still want to leave after that, I promise I will never bother you about it again. And I didn't want to say anything, but it is my birthday."

Jojo dropped her head. "Okay. I'll be there." Her mouth was set in a hard line. "I was going to hang out with Oona, Luna, Joie, and Twyla—you know those are really their names, by the way—but I guess I could do that Sunday. But this is the last time, Ralph."

As he watched her stomp off, Ralph smiled to himself, feeling proud of how he'd handled the encounter. But something nagged at him. He had to admit the only way he'd gotten Jojo to come was by using guilt, and that was nothing to be proud of. Well, once the game started, he knew she'd come around. He just had to create the coolest story ever.

A GOLDEN GIFT

It was Friday afternoon, and Ralph was feeling both anxious and sad. In the good old pre-braces days, this had been his favorite time of the week. But instead of planning a great adventure, all the way home, Ralph worried about how to keep his friends from deserting the game.

One issue was that the three hours usually seemed to speed by, with almost no time to really get anything going.

So his first job, he decided, was to get them to spend more time there Saturday. He knew if he had just a few more hours, he could get the magic back.

He had to start at dinner, getting his parents on board.

His mom was more interested in telling him that something had arrived in the mail for him. Had he ordered something and not told them?

It was from the RoDCon. Just check-in information, probably. Right now he was less excited about going to the convention all alone. Maybe if things went well, he could get a couple of his friends to change their minds and come with him.

"How are you getting there Sunday?" his mother asked.

"I was just going to walk," said Ralph. "It's like right there at the Beveren."

The Beveren was a fancy hotel that had opened up in downtown Brooklyn.

His mother looked worried, but his father looked over at her. "He's turning twelve. Maybe we should let him go."

"No fair," said his sister GG, spearing an asparagus. "When I was twelve, you never let me do anything."

"Which we had to hear about every night," her father. "So maybe, just maybe, letting Ralph go will spare us that experience again."

"Speaking of getting older . . . ," Ralph began. This was the perfect segue into his plan. "This might just be the last session ever of RoD—"

"Well, we'll have to find something else for you to get involved with," said his dad.

They seemed almost relieved! It was totally frustrating. It was as if they thought the other kids had it right, moving on to other interests, and Ralph was the one who was clinging to some immature waste of time. Okay, maybe they didn't say that, but it sure felt that way. "I want to keep playing Reign of Dragons."

"Remember how into Legos you were? It was Lego all the time," his mother reminded him. "Where are all your Lego kits now? Under your bed."

"This is different," groused Ralph. "I just want to keep playing Reign of Dragons. What's wrong with that?"

"Nothing, sweetheart," his mother said. "It's only that it seems your friends aren't as into it as you are."

"Maybe it's temporary," suggested GG. "You know, stop it

for a while and then see if you're still into it in like six months. You might find it's just not the same thing. Like when I was obsessed with Barbies."

"You were nine!" Ralph said, trying not to yell at the dinner table.

"Don't yell at the dinner table," admonished his mother. So much for that.

His sister glared at him. This wasn't good. He needed an ally.

Ralph turned to his dad. "You should understand, Dad. Weren't you into anything fun when you were my age?"

His father thought for a minute. "I made models. That was kind of cool. I remember spending an entire summer making a *Millennium Falcon* when I was twelve."

Ralph turned to his mom. "See? He was twelve. How long did you make models?"

His dad grinned. "Well, right after that I discovered girls. And music. So making models became less important."

Ralph threw his head back and looked at the ceiling. He had taken some serious damage to his mental health points with that one.

"Nobody is saying you have to stop," GG said, "but how are you going to keep it going if all your friends are leaving?"

It was time to move in and strike the first blow. "Here's what I'm hoping. I've asked for an extra-long session. Like until dinner. I'm hoping if I make the story good enough, they'll stay."

His mother raised her eyebrows. "You know tomorrow's shoot is a long one. We're going to be gone all day. So it's up to your sister. If she wants to hang out here for six hours . . ."

"No way," his sister said. "That's not going to happen in this lifetime. I mean, I know this is a fantasy game, but that is a total fantasy."

This dealt even more damage. Ralph had to counter this with a critical hit.

"How about this," he suggested. "You want to study for the SATs right? And Melora lives three houses away."

Melora was GG's best friend. And Ralph knew they loved to hang out together. So what if they spent half the time watching cooking videos. If his parents thought they were studying for the SATs, that wasn't his problem. It was his weapon.

GG brightened. "Yeah, right. The SATs. We really need to practice this weekend."

Ralph turned to his parents. "So can she go to Melora's? She'll only be three houses away. I have my phone. There's not going to be any kind of emergency or anything anyway. We're just going to be playing the game the whole time."

Ralph's mom turned to GG. "So you'd be there the whole time? No going into the city or anything like that?"

"Mom, I said I'd be there. I mean, at most, maybe we'd go out for a slice of pizza for lunch or something."

"Perfect," said Ralph's dad, who was more of the producer of the two of them. He tended to focus on the logistics, so he was on board already. "And there's food in the fridge, so your friends won't starve. Sounds like a plan."

Ralph could feel his mental health points filling back up. Now for step two: getting the others to agree to stay.

"So you'll text the other parents?" he asked his mom.

"Yes, I'll let them know it's okay."

As Ralph helped GG clear the table and load the

dishwasher, his mom would periodically call out that one or another of his friends had agreed to stay on for the extra time. The final text was from Jojo's mom, who said she'd be there and that Jojo was looking forward to it.

Ralph knew this was garbage. Jojo's mom was just being nice, but he didn't care. Victory was his.

He headed to his room, grabbing the padded envelope from RoDCon. As he plopped down on his bed, he heard the package rattle like a box of dice. Ralph had dozens of sets of dice and one more wouldn't make a difference, but still, it was a nice bit of swag. He emptied the contents onto his bed. There was a note and an oblong box. Usually dice boxes were translucent plastic so you could see the color of the dice you were buying. They came in all sorts of colors, and each player had their favorites. Jojo liked ebony, Noel always brought his marbleized fancy dice (which he kept in a velvet pouch), Cammi favored purple, and Persephone insisted on rolling her lucky hot pinks. Ralph was the only one who wasn't particular. He was also the only one with multiple sets. This set, however, was covered in black paper. He turned to the note.

Congratulations! As one of the members of the Search for the Seven Serpent Scepter Forum who has completed the first six quests, you are eligible for the RoDCon RoD contest. Ralph rolled his eyes at the cheesy name but continued. *Seven of the boxes of dice we have sent out contain 1 (one) golden die. If you receive a golden die, you are entitled to participate in the special game of Reign of Dragons held at the convention at high noon, GM'd by none other than Andy Wycroft, the famed "first player" himself!*

That was something. More than just a new set of dice, at least! If he won. When Warwick had first designed the game, he had tested it with his own children, with Andy creating the first character ever in the game, a dwarf called MiniChin. Playing with him would almost be like playing with Wycroft himself.

Ralph tore off the black paper and saw that each die was also covered in paper. It was a little much, if you asked him. "They're really amping up the suspense," he said to himself, shaking his head.

He laboriously unwrapped one die after another, revealing d4s and d8s and a d12, all in different bright shades. Then he got to the d20. It felt heavier than the others.

Ralph paused.

He'd never liked *Charlie and the Chocolate Factory*. They'd read it in school, and he always thought it was a little cheesy that after pages and pages of poor starving Charlie not getting anything, he magically found one of the golden tickets. It all seemed too corny to him.

But here he was. He knew before he'd even opened it that he was having his own Charlie Bucket moment.

He carefully peeled the paper away to reveal the golden d20.

17

RPG GETS TO THE POINT

"So you think it's real gold?" Noel was weighing it in his hand. "You know, we can find out. My dad has stuff at the house we could use to test it."

"I doubt it," said Ralph, eyeing the front door for the thousandth time in the last five minutes. It was now twelve-fifteen, and so far only Noel had shown up.

Ralph glanced at the coffee table in front of him. He'd wanted everything to be perfect. With GG gone, he'd moved the game to their spacious living room on the parlor floor instead of the cramped area downstairs. He'd gotten everyone's favorite snacks and arranged them in bowls (except for the red licorice Jojo loved, which he had carefully placed in what he hoped was a particularly festive arrangement on a plate in front of where she usually sat).

"Did anybody say anything to you?" asked Ralph.

Noel carefully put the golden die down and thought. "Well, Jojo told me this was all a waste of time and how annoying you were in front of her friends. Does that count?" He said it with broad smile, as if Ralph would somehow find this funny. Noel just didn't get it, so there was no use being annoyed with him. He just told it like it was.

"That's ridiculous. I was just standing there waiting for them to finish. And she's the one who wanted to talk to me."

"Maybe your just standing there was what was so annoying," said Noel, taking one of the licorice vines.

"That's for Jojo," Ralph said. "I got the corn chips for you."

Noel regarded the licorice. "I don't see her name on it. Anyway, she might not come, so what's the difference?"

Ralph slumped into his chair at the head of the table, where he had hoped to lead his group into an adventure so compelling they'd demand to keep going. But that meant they had to show up.

The doorbell suddenly began frantically ringing. Ralph leapt up and tore open the door. To his vast relief, Jojo pushed past him, closely followed by Persephone and Cammi, who looked even more distraught than usual. "I'm so, so sorry, Ralph. Jojo and Perseph were at a sleepover at my house and we kind of got up late. And then my mom couldn't find her keys, and—"

"Don't worry about it," Ralph assured him. "I'm just glad you got here."

Jojo was texting someone already. Ralph had a bad feeling about this. He considered giving her some licorice as a peace offering. But that wasn't right, because they weren't fighting. At least, as far as he knew. But then, he didn't think he had been annoying, so what did he know?

It was worth a try. "Umm . . . Jojo? Look! I got you licorice! This is the kind you like, right?"

Jojo glanced up from her phone. "Um . . . liked. I'm kind of off processed sugar right now. I need to eat healthy for meets."

"That's funny, I saw you sharing a bag of gummy bears with Oona and Luna in study hall," Noel said, clueless as always.

"Those weren't gummy bears, Noel. They were carrot sticks."

"Yeah, right. Carrot sticks." Noel laughed.

"They were. Are you calling me a liar?" Jojo looked like she was ready to throw her phone at Noel's head.

"Jojo, chill out. Noel is just being Noel," Ralph said. "If you say they were carrot sticks, they were carrot sticks."

Jojo went back to her phone.

Cammi and Persephone were talking about an episode of *High School a Cappella,* a show they were both devoted to. It was all about high school drama and who had a crush on whom, and then at some point there would be a musical number and all the kids would start singing. Ralph had tried to get into it, but it all seemed kind of silly to him.

Cammi and his girlfriends would watch the episodes over and over again, quoting lines from the show and even writing stories about the characters falling in love with each other, sometimes boys with boys and girls with girls. Ralph thought an orc falling in love with a human (like Persephone's character's parents) was a lot more interesting.

Persephone noticed the golden die. Her eyes lit up. "That's so pretty! Did you get a new set?"

"Yeah, but that one is special," said Ralph.

"Pick it up," Noel suggested. "We were wondering if it was real gold."

Persephone cradled it in her two tiny hands. "Wow. It's really heavy. Where did you get it?"

"It's quite a story," Ralph began, relishing the moment. Even Jojo had looked up from her phone. "You see—"

"Warwick Wycroft's son sent it to him!" Noel broke in.

"What?" asked Cammi. "That's amazing!"

Ralph glared at Noel. "Can I please tell it?"

"You always take too long with your stories," said Noel, in his Noel way.

"Anyway. I was online and registering for the RoDCon—which I asked all of you to go to with me, but anyway—and there was this picture in the corner of the screen of this weird guy dressed all in black with long hair—"

"Warwick Wycroft's son," Noel added helpfully.

"Fine, you tell it."

"No, we want to hear you tell it," Persephone insisted.

"I thought I always take too long," Ralph groused.

Jojo put her phone away. "Just tell your stupid story and let's get going."

"Okay. So this envelope came in the mail with a free set of dice. Of course, I need another set of dice like I need another sister, but—"

"Get to the point!" said Jojo through gritted teeth.

"Sorry. So anyway, there's a piece of paper with a picture of the same guy, and it turns out because we'd gotten to the sixth scepter we were eligible to get—shut up, Noel—one of seven gold dice hidden among probably a hundred boxes they sent out, and if you get one, they fly you to RoDCon to play at a special game. So I waited until I came home and then—"

"Wait, so who was in the picture?" asked Cammi.

"Andy Wycroft, Warwick Wycroft's son!" said Ralph.

"You didn't say that," Noel said. "All you said was—"

"I thought it was obvious," Ralph said, closing his eyes.

"He could have been just one of the organizers," Jojo said, taking a piece of the red licorice. Ralph didn't say anything.

"I thought you weren't eating those," said you-know-who.

"Shut up, Noel." Jojo glared.

"Can I finish my story?" said Ralph. "I said he'd invited me, remember?"

"Actually, Noel said that," Persephone reminded him.

"I went upstairs," Ralph pressed on, determined to get to the punch line, "and after dinner, I opened the package."

"Is that part relevant?" asked Jojo, who was now on her third Red Vine.

"At least he didn't tell us what he had for dinner," Persephone said.

"That's true," said Cammi.

Ralph grabbed the die. "Forget it. You guys clearly don't care."

"Stop being dramatic," said Persephone, which was enough to make everyone else crack up, considering the source.

"I mean it. Nobody wants to be here but me." Ralph could feel his lower lip starting to tremble. He really didn't want to cry in front of his friends, but it had finally dawned on him.

Cammi immediately rushed over and hugged him. Which

only made things worse. Now he was taking deep breaths and could feel the tears forming in his eyes. He'd worked so hard on the adventure for today, all for nothing.

Even Jojo softened. "Ralph . . . RPG, don't be silly. Come on. We want to be here. . . . It's just . . ."

"Oh please. You want to go shopping with your real friends," Ralph said, realizing how stupid it sounded when he said it out loud.

Jojo set her jaw in a firm line. "Ralph. I'm not going to apologize for having other friends. So does Cammi. And Persephone."

"And me too! Lots of other friends. I even have friends online. There's a kid who lives in Holland I met while playing *Rocket Fighter*," Noel added, helpful as always.

Persephone handed Ralph a tissue and he wiped his eyes and blew his nose. "I know. I just . . . wanted it to be important to you guys, and—"

"We're here, aren't we?" said Jojo. "Let's just play the game already."

They gathered around the table.

"I never finished my story," Ralph said.

"Oh, for crying out loud!" screamed Jojo.

"I want to hear it," said Cammi softly.

"Me too. But the quick version," said Persephone. "Like one sentence."

"Fine. I opened it up and after unwrapping the other six dice, I ended up unwrapping this one and finding out I was a winner."

There was a pause.

"Wow, that was pretty undramatic," Noel said.

Cammi jumped in. "I think it's cool. You're going to play at RoDCon! I wish I could go!"

"Me too!" said Jojo.

"You are such a liar," Ralph said, grinning.

"Okay, so I don't want to go all that much," Jojo admitted.

"I would go if we didn't have rehearsal," said Persephone, "just to see all those people dressed up in their costumes."

Everyone settled in.

18

ALEA IACTA EST

"Shouldn't we remind ourselves of where we are in the story?" asked Cammi.

"Of course. So we are ... deep beneath the mountain Morgorath, within the ancient stones of the Temple of Kamach'Ldar, and just as the Kreel army was defeated, the Komach'Kreel appeared."

Four faces leaned in. Ralph felt the familiar rush of the game come back as they assumed their characters.

"You have never seen anything like it. Monstrous, towering twelve feet above you and encased in some sort of enchanted armor, the giant demon unleashes his barbed tail and swipes at you."

Ralph turned to Jojo. Her eyes were shining. "What do you do?"

"I strike at his tail with my sword," Jojo said confidently.

"Jandia takes her sword in two hands and swings the mighty Strach'Klan, already stained with the blood of dozens of Kreel dead. Roll for damage," Ralph instructed, to discover what, if anything, the blow had done.

Jojo rolled her own d20. Her face lit up. "Eighteen!"

"The blow glances off the scales of the monster's tail, leaving no mark."

"What?" protested Jojo. "I rolled an eighteen! That should have cut the tail off!"

"It can't have left no damage," added Cammi. "She's a Level Twenty warrior."

"Jandia's broadsword should have been able to take down any monster with a roll like that," said Persephone.

Noel had snuck a glance at the notes Ralph was using. "Wow. Guys, I don't think there's any way we can defeat that thing. Its numbers are way too high."

"So what do we do?" asked Cammi.

"That is completely unfair," said Persephone. "We have to be able to defeat it."

"I'm sorry, guys," Ralph said. "I think Noel is right. I didn't write these stats. They came straight from Warwick Wycroft. And it's the Komach'Kreel's turn."

"So we're just going to all die here?" wailed Persephone.

"In all our years playing, we've never had a TPK," said Noel grimly.

That was true. In RoD, a TPK, or total party kill, was the worst thing that could happen. It was the end of the game. Occasionally in a game, one member might lose enough health points to die along the way, but as a cleric with special healing skills, Ralph was always able to bring them back to life. But this monster was too powerful for even his healing abilities.

As he checked the monster's stats again, Ralph saw a small footnote, marked with a light golden *z*. He'd read this page a dozen times, and he could have sworn it hadn't been there before.

"Hold on a second, guys," Ralph said. "There's something else here."

Ralph looked at the end of his pages where the notes were. He got to the last page, where the note was *y*. Then as he rubbed the page, as if they were stuck together, a thin last page pulled itself away from the others. On it, in a different font, was written:

An alcove appears behind you.

Ralph read this out loud to the group.

"We run behind the alcove!" shouted Noel as the others nodded.

Ralph rolled the dice for the monster. It came up 2. "The Komach'Kreel is temporarily confused. It can smell you, hear your heartbeats. It comes closer. . . ."

He turned to Noel. "So what are you going to do? Bram?"

Noel thought for a moment. "Can I give my turn to the wizard?"

Ralph frowned and checked the rule book. "I guess so. If you want."

Noel whispered something in Cammi's ear.

Cammi nodded and smiled. "I cast the Portal Awakening spell. It takes us to another dimensional plane."

Ralph checked his book. The Portal Awakening spell was a brilliant move.

"Gerontius casts Portal Awakening. The very air around you shifts. If the spell is successful, you will be taken to another world, where who knows what mysteries and dangers might await. For this spell, the GM rolls the dice."

Ralph picked up the d20.

They all knew what was coming next. It was a little ritual Declan had taught them. Before he would roll as GM, he would say a Latin phrase that was first spoken by Julius Caesar before he crossed the Rubicon River and faced his destiny to challenge the Republic and become emperor. *Alea iacta est*. It translates to "The die is cast." Meaning that there is no going back.

As Ralph rubbed the golden d20 in his hands, it seemed to vibrate. Pulsate.

"Alea iacta est," intoned Ralph "The die is cast!"

He threw the golden die onto the table, where it rolled slowly and came to a stop.

Twenty.

"A portal has opened, and . . . ," Ralph began, but stopped.

"Do you feel that?" asked Noel.

"How can we not?" demanded Jojo.

The entire room seemed to be vibrating.

"Are they doing construction outside?" Cammi suggested. When they were working on the street, the apartment did often shake. But this was different.

"What's that?" asked Persephone.

There was a low humming, and the room was definitely shaking. The air around them shimmered as the lights seemed to grow brighter and brighter.

"What's happening?" yelled Noel, his voice almost drowned out by a sound that replaced the humming. The new sound was like nothing they'd ever heard, a tearing apart, a blazing combination of cries and roars and rushing air pulling at them, getting louder and louder.

PART TWO

19

THE SPELL IS CAST

The soulless yellow eyes of the Komach'Kreel darted about, the black slits of its pupils taking in the carnage of the ruined temple. Bodies of dead Kreel littered the altar.

Hissing, it prowled the ancient structure, knocking the fluted columns over with each twitch of its massive barbed tail.

The adventurers huddled in a nearby alcove, watching it. Jandia Ravenhelm had lost her bloodlust, leaving her sullen and confused. She had fought and defeated enemies of all shapes and sizes, but this creature was unlike anything she had ever encountered. She barely registered Torgrim's low mutterings as he cast his most powerful healing spell on her battered arm.

Softly, Mirak was singing a melody that both soothed Jandia and helped speed the cleric's spell. She watched as the muscles and sinews of the barbarian warrior's arm knit together and the skin formed over it. It was extraordinary. But right now, it came as more of a relief. If they were to have any chance at all to destroy the demon, they would need Jandia's strong arms and two-handed blade.

As the sounds of the creature neared, the elf and halfling were deep in counsel together. "There is great sense in what you propose, Halfling." Gerontius Darksbane knelt to speak softly to Bram. "But there is great danger as well."

"It is too powerful to fight," hissed Bram.

Jandia grunted, her healing complete. She gripped her sword, testing her newly healed bicep. "You do good work, Cleric," she allowed. "I am ready to bring down the enemy or die in the trying."

"You shall do no such thing," Gerontius said as he strode over and put a hand on Jandia's sword arm. "We have an idea." He gestured to his spellbook.

"Whatever you have in mind, please enlighten us," said the bard, pulling an arrow from her quiver, "as the time approaches for action. The creature is only a few steps away."

"And we have no avenue of escape," added Torgrim.

"A fancy way of saying we are trapped," chuckled Bram, "but traps can be thwarted."

Gerontius ignored them, paging through the well-worn pages of his spellbook, humming slightly to himself.

"He has the air of someone with all the time in the world," growled Jandia, "when our lives could well be measured in seconds."

There was a burst of flame. The Komach'Kreel was growing quite near.

Gerontius held out his hand. "Take hold, Barbarian. And each of you do likewise. We must all keep this connection, no matter what happens."

Torgrim grabbed Jandia's hand in his and extended his other to Bram, who took it greedily and turned to Mirak, who looked down at the halfling's outstretched offering.

"That hand is as slippery as they come, Rogue, liberating purses and escaping the grip of constables. Make sure it holds mine fast."

She gripped it, and the spell began its work. The orb in Gerontius's hand glowed brighter, gaining strength as the wizard chanted the final words of the Astral Transport incantation.

The air about them began to shimmer just as the Komach'Kreel finally found them, roaring so deep and loud the ground beneath their feet shook. It grinned in victory, before howling in fury as it watched the party fade into nothingness.

THE NEW WORLD

Although Gerontius had traveled from one plane to another before, he had never gotten used to it. It occurred to him that perhaps he should have warned the others as he felt the usual sensation of being pulled apart from all sides, of thousands of tiny fingers picking at him. His eyes were closed, but he could sense the terror coursing through the others.

Jandia clung to Gerontius's hand with a desperation heretofore unknown to her. Barbarians know no fear in the face of the enemy, but this was a faceless foe, pulling them tumbling and lurching through an unremitting blackness.

Slowly, the vibrations buffeting their bodies seemed to subside, and the darkness began to fade. Their senses grasped for the familiar, anything to do with the corporeal world, a world with substance and sound, not the empty void they had been traveling through. Then their feet found purchase, and it appeared they had arrived at their destination, wherever that was.

Jandia was the first to speak. "Is it safe to open our eyes?"

"I believe so, but take care. I don't know where we transported to," answered Gerontius.

"It sounds quiet," murmured Mirak. "Perhaps we have come to safety."

Torgrim pushed his helmet up over his brow and opened his eyes. "We are not in Demos."

"You are as wise as ever, Dwarf," snorted Bram, "for stating the obvious."

They had landed, it appeared, in a small chamber, perhaps ten feet by ten feet. The ceiling was high, and there was an unlit fireplace on the wall facing them. Paintings of unknown lands were hanging on the walls, and the room was furnished with finely wrought couches and chairs.

"This is no cottage," said Torgrim.

Jandia raised her nose. "I smell food." She gestured to a long table before them, littered with papers, yellow sticks of wood, and mysterious-looking books with bright pictures of dragons and fighters and wizards on their covers. And there were bowls filled with food like none they had ever seen—puffy white little globes and red thickly corded strands, as well as thin yellow triangles.

Bram reached down to try one before his hand was slapped away by Mirak. "We do not know if this is poison. What if it's a feast left for the gods?"

Torgrim stroked his beard and took in the rest of the chamber. He turned to the others.

"Which god or goddess this may serve, I do not know. But I do know this." He pointed to the far corner of the room, where five small beings were cowering. "We are not alone."

UNEXPECTED GUESTS

The vibrations had stopped, and Ralph opened his eyes. He wondered if this was what it was like to be unconscious. Clearly what he was seeing couldn't be there. He was vaguely aware of bodies pressing against his, but he was frozen in place with the thought that if he simply waited, things would return to normal. For what felt like a long time, nothing moved, and an eerie quiet settled over the room.

Then the silence was broken. "Are you seeing what I'm seeing?" It was the unmistakable creak of Noel's voice.

"Ye-e-s." Jojo. Sounding very un-Jojo-like.

"What's going on?" quavered Cammi.

"RPG? What did you do?" Persephone was shaking him, pulling his arm.

Ralph turned to the others. He saw his own fear and confusion mirrored in their faces. "I'm not sure. . . . There has to be some explanation. . . . I mean, there has to be . . ."

Across the room, there was the low buzz of voices. Ralph

looked over to try to make sense of the five beings now standing in the entry to the living room of his family's apartment.

One of them appeared to be about their age, as he was as small as they were. But he had long sideburns elegantly shaped along his high cheekbones and carried himself like an adult. He had a braid going down his back, a pointed nose, and a small smile on his face as his eyes darted about the room.

He was dressed simply, in a white shirt with a brown leather vest fastened with what looked like brass buckles. Embroidered on the vest was a pattern of tree branches and birds. His pants were brown leggings, stitched rudely on the sides. His belt held a small pouch and two scabbards, with a dagger in each. One had a white handle, the other black.

Next to him was one of the most imposing figures Ralph had ever seen.

It was a tall woman, balancing on the balls of her feet, her eyes fiery and fierce. Her rippling muscles were barely covered by the protective leather sleeves on her arms and by shin guards. She had a few pieces of rude cloth covering her top and below her waist, leaving her impressive abdomen and thighs bare. Her mane of thick red hair was pulled back and held in place with a scrap of animal hide with a bone through it.

What caught the eye first, though, was her scarlet cape, held at her throat by a gold clasp in the shape of a raven's head. Well, that and the gigantic two-handed sword she was holding up in front of her.

"Stay your sword, Barbarian," he heard a cool voice say.

The owner of the voice was a tall, elegant woman standing next to the swordswoman. Clad in a bright blue tunic with runes stitched through it and fine silk tights, she carried a bow, and strapped to her back appeared to be a quiver of arrows and some sort of small harp. Her jet-black hair was streaked with gray and cascaded down her back freely. Her arched eyebrows and bright blue eyes made her look quite beautiful, until you looked down and saw the fanglike lower canine teeth jutting out of her jaw.

A grunt came from next to her.

There was another little man, but unlike the lithe and graceful first one, he was burly and thick-necked, with bushy eyebrows and black eyes glowering under his simple helmet. He had a finely braided beard, with a bulbous nose above it. He wore chain mail, and beaten metal armor encased his lower body and legs. In his left hand was a huge and fearsome mallet-like hammer covered in metal studs. A great gold medallion hung around his neck.

"Wizard, this is your doing. Are they friend or foe?" he growled.

The person he was addressing was slim and pale, with fog-gray hair forming a widow's peak on his brow, pulled back to reveal sharply pointed ears. His lips were thin, and his slightly upturned eyes looked bemused. He wore a moss-green robe, secured tightly with a silver clasp in the shape of a leaf. Visible below the robe were beautifully tooled leather boots. Over all was a hooded cloak of a darker shade of green, which was thrown back to reveal a beautifully wrought curved sword in the graceful elvish style. What looked like a very old book, with brass on each corner, hung from a belt around his waist.

"Perhaps we shall do well to ask," the man in green said simply.

21

WHAT IN THE WORLD?

The small wiry man in brown took a few steps toward Ralph and the others. He peered at them and called back to his companions. "They seem to be human younglings. At least, this is how they have chosen to appear to us."

"Okay, this is officially weird," said Persephone. "What is going on?"

The man in brown bowed to them. He held his hands open, as if to show he held no weapon. "We are travelers from another place. Do you understand?"

While the others just nodded, Ralph heard himself say, "Yes, we understand. Please excuse us for a moment, will you?"

He backed his way toward the sliding doors that led out of the living room, the others close on his heels. The five intruders watched them, with expressions ranging from smiles (the small man and the one they called "Wizard") to scowls (the scary-looking woman and the little guy with the crazy beard). Ralph smiled back, closed the sliding doors, and faced the others.

Jojo had pulled out her phone. "I'm calling 911."

"Wait," said Noel, "we don't know who they are."

"Did you see that sword?" asked Persephone, eyes wide. "I'm with Jojo."

"They didn't make us stay there," reasoned Noel. "Don't you think if they were criminals, they wouldn't just let us walk out like this?"

"Um, I don't want to get off track," Cammi said quietly, "but what was up with those costumes?"

Ralph nodded. "So there's a clue right there. I mean, that's some pretty serious cosplay going on there."

"Maybe they're here from RoDCon," said Noel. "Like, when you rolled the dice it sends out a signal and they're here to award you with something. Like they found you through GPS."

"Yeah, but how would they get here immediately?" scoffed Jojo. "They didn't even ring the doorbell."

"Maybe GG left the door open when she went to Melora's, so they decided to make a dramatic entrance," Noel insisted. He was not going to let go of this theory, Ralph decided, until someone came up with something better.

"So you think they're actors hired by RoD?" asked Persephone.

"What other possible explanation could there be?" said Noel triumphantly.

There was the sound of voices inside. Ralph shrugged and was about to open the door when Cammi stopped him.

"Did you guys notice anything about them?" he asked.

Jojo shot him a look. "You mean other than the whole costumes and swords and that humongous hammer that one guy is carrying?"

Cammi turned to Ralph. "Exactly. The war hammer Deathbringer. Isn't that what Torgrim carries?"

"Lots of dwarf characters carry hammers," Ralph said.

"The wizard is an elf, with a silver leaf clasp, and I know that Jandia has a scarlet cape and a two-handed sword."

"You mean they're dressed as our characters?" Ralph said, trying not to laugh. "They're just generic . . . you know, typical . . ."

"No, I think Cammi's right. A bard, a cleric, a wizard, a barbarian, and a halfling rogue . . . ," Persephone said, counting them off on her fingers. "You think that's a coincidence?"

"Those are definitely our characters!" said Noel.

"You just said—" Ralph groused.

"I've changed my mind!" Noel said. "That was a stupid idea."

"At least we agree on that," Jojo said.

"Isn't today your birthday, RPG?" Noel asked, ignoring Jojo.

"My birthday . . . ," Ralph said. "Oh . . . you don't think . . ."

Noel smiled in triumph. "Sure. Your parents hired them as a surprise."

"But they don't know anything about the game," Ralph said, "so how would they—"

"Declan," Cammi said, nodding. "He could have given them all the information."

"It's true. Plus, your parents produce commercials," Jojo

said. "Putting together something like this would be nothing for them. The whole thing is probably being taped."

Of course.

The whole "We're gone all day" thing. They were probably hiding somewhere in the house, filming right now.

"So they're actors!" said Persephone delightedly. "Awesome!"

Before Ralph could stop her, she flung open the doors.

The one dressed as the wizard was leafing through the book on his belt. The dwarf and the one with the harp were at the window, peering out, mesmerized. The halfling was looking intently at the photos on the mantel, and the large-muscled woman was kneeling by the coffee table. She had picked up the bowl of popcorn and was smelling it curiously.

Jojo approached her. "You can have some snacks if you want."

Jandia peered at her suspiciously. "Snax? This is to eat, yes?"

"Boy, you really stay in character," said Jojo. "Um, yes, it is to eat."

Jandia picked up one popped kernel and looked at it. She turned to the dwarf. "Should I try it?"

The dwarf approached the bowl and put his hand in. "Um, maybe you should wash your hands first," suggested Ralph as he caught a whiff of something. It smelled like Torgrim hadn't bathed in months. Where did his parents find these people?

Torgrim stared at the boy in front of him and grinned. "I will not need to purify my hands for this. It will either kill me or not." He shoved a handful in his mouth and proceeded to produce disgusting crunching noises. He nodded to the others.

"It is good!" he proclaimed.

"It would be a boon," said the one with the harp, "if you would swallow what is in your mouth before making such statements."

Persephone tugged at her sleeve. "Um, excuse me, you're Mirak, right?"

The bard looked down in amazement. "How is it you know my name?"

The rogue looked over from the mantel. "Perhaps your fame as a singer of great songs has traveled so far and wide as to make it into this dimension."

"Something like that," Persephone said. She leaned in conspiratorially. "So how did you get this job? Did you audition?"

Mirak looked confused. "This job? If by that you mean how came me to join this company, that is a long and exciting tale, which begins at my birth. Where it was foretold—"

"She will continue for an hour or more if you wish," broke in the halfling. "I think it far more interesting to hear about you younglings."

Here it comes, thought Ralph. They're going to ask about the birthday boy and do something corny.

The wizard looked up. "Yes, if we were called to this place, it would be good to learn more about it."

The more Ralph looked at them, the more impressed he was. His parents must have spent a fortune on these costumes and props, let alone finding actors to play these roles in full

· 122 ·

facial prosthetic makeup. He was waiting for GG and his folks to jump out and say, "Surprise!"

"So do you work out in a gym?" Jojo was asking Jandia. "I bet you're a personal trainer, right?"

Jandia was licking the popcorn bowl. "These words are strange to me. I am a fighter."

"Yeah, yeah, I know. Barbarian fighter, level twenty, blah blah blah," Jojo said.

Jandia let out a low growl.

"It is never wise to mock barbarians," counseled the wizard. "Most unwise indeed."

Cammi looked enchanted by Gerontius's cloak. He reached out tentatively. "May I?"

"Of course," answered the wizard gently.

Cammi rubbed it between his fingers. It seemed to melt at his touch, it was so fine.

"I've never seen fabric like this," he said to his friends. "It's so cool. I wonder what it's made of?"

"It is fairy-woven," said the wizard, "by the good folk of Cloverdell. Of cobwebs is it made, and moonflowers and—"

"—woodbine leaves and sweetbriar," Cammi almost whispered.

"You know your feywork well, youngling!"

Cammi looked up, trembling. "You . . . couldn't know that. How did you know that?"

He fell to the floor. The other kids rushed to him.

The cleric pushed them aside. "I am a healer. Let me minister to him."

This had gone far enough. Ralph looked up at these

· 123 ·

strangers in his house. "Okay, the show's over. You can stop now."

Persephone held Cammi's head in her arms. He was staring, wide-eyed. "No one knew that. . . ."

"What?" asked Persephone.

"No one, not Declan, not anyone. I never told anyone what Gerontius's cloak was made of," Cammi said solemnly. "And that isn't any fabric I've ever seen. And I've seen pretty much everything in my grandma's costume shop. If it's cloth, they've used it."

Ralph felt his breaths coming faster and his heart beating harder.

"You must have told him and forgotten," Noel said. "It happens. I mean—"

"He got that cloak when he won that challenge in Waterspout," Ralph remembered. "That was after Declan left."

"Then you told your parents," Noel said, a little louder. "Right? What other explanation is there?"

Ralph shook his head. He never told them a thing.

"You know of the challenge?" asked Gerontius. "How do you know this?"

"That's easy," Noel said. "RPG is the one who—"

Ralph stopped him. "Your exploits are known even here."

He tried his best to bow without looking too stupid. "Would you excuse us once more? I must confer with my compatriots."

"Of course!" answered Gerontius.

"Anything we can get you?" asked Persephone as the others led the still-shaken Cammi out of the room.

"More snax!" demanded Jandia, tugging on a Red Vine.

The children retreated, and the doors slid shut.

There was the sound of laughter from the corner. Bram looked at Gerontius and laughed again. "These younglings are either very wise or powerful or both. I think we have found a good place."

22

WHEN NOTHING IS LEFT
BUT THE IMPOSSIBLE

Ralph looked at his friends. He was pretty sure he looked just as shocked and frightened as the rest of them, but he was going to do his best to figure this out. "So, any other ideas?"

"Mass hypnosis?" suggested Noel.

"Oh, please," said Persephone. "Why would someone do that? And how would they do it?"

"We don't know," Noel said triumphantly, "because we're hypnotized."

Jojo pinched his arm, hard.

"Ow! What gives!" protested Noel.

"I was trying to wake you up," she said, smiling.

Cammi spoke, his voice barely a whisper. "You don't think it's possible—"

"That they are, like, real? Like from another dimension or something?" snorted Noel.

"You don't have to be so snotty about it," Persephone said, holding Cammi's hand.

"We made them up," Ralph insisted. "I mean, we did. It's just . . . impossible. This isn't Narnia. It's Brooklyn."

"Actually, a lot of fantasy books take place in Brooklyn," Noel said. "I was just reading one about vampires."

"Whatever," said Jojo, crossing her arms. "This is stupid. They can't really be from another world. Things like that don't happen."

"But wouldn't it be cool if they did?" mused Persephone.

They thought about that for a moment.

"I . . . I don't know what to think," said Noel finally. For the first time he seemed unsure of himself.

"Your dad's a scientist," Ralph said. "What would he say? Wouldn't he insist that there's a logical explanation for all this?"

Noel looked back toward the living room. "Actually, he likes to say there are all sorts of things science just can't explain."

"That doesn't make them magic," insisted Ralph.

"Then what is it?" demanded Persephone.

Ralph thought for a minute. He thought of rolling the dice, of the spell, of all the possibilities they had rejected. "I guess that's for us to find out, right?"

He pulled back the sliding door quickly, and the halfling, who was leaning on the door, fell into them. He'd been listening on the other side. Instead of hitting the floor, he did a graceful roll and flipped back onto his feet.

Persephone and Cammi applauded and he bowed.

"He does have a high dexterity score," remembered Ralph.

"Jandia is becoming hungrier," Bram said, looking around.

"Come on, the kitchen is this way," said Ralph, pushing him across the dining room.

Bram had paused in front of the kitchen. He carefully put a hand out and drew it back quickly. He then dipped a toe into the room and gingerly tapped the floor.

"What the heck are you doing?" asked Ralph.

Bram looked at him and raised a warning hand. "Checking for traps, of course. You have much to learn, young human. Never enter a room without checking for traps. We rogues are especially good at this."

"Yes, I know!" said Ralph, pushing past him. "But it's my house. There are no traps here."

"What's the fun of that?" asked Bram, following close behind.

Ralph loaded himself down with everything that looked vaguely snacklike.

Whenever his parents did a commercial shoot, they brought home stuff from the craft services table, which was the free food table set up for the cast and crew. There were always bowls of fruit and fiber bars and wedges of cheese left over at the end of the day. He got out a tray and was about to hand it to Bram, who was busying himself pocketing silverware from one of the drawers.

"Put those back!" ordered Ralph. "They don't belong to you."

Bram looked crestfallen. He emptied his pockets. "Not even one of these?" He held up a bread knife.

"Just put it on the tray. We can use it to cut the cheese."

Bram sighed and did what he was told. It was odd. Ralph didn't think the rogue usually listened in the game when someone told him not to steal.

They walked back into the living room, to find Torgrim and Gerontius deep in conversation with Noel. Persephone and Cammi were admiring Mirak's harp.

Jandia stood apart, glowering, but she brightened when she saw the tray of food.

She reached over and took a handful of grapes and shoved them in her mouth, then took about half the cheese.

"She doesn't have the best manners, does she?" whispered Ralph.

"I wouldn't bring that up," counseled Bram. "The last person to do so found his head severed from his body."

"Good point." Ralph nodded.

Jojo stood by the barbarian, looking protective. "Maybe she's just hangry."

Bram looked puzzled. "I do not know this word."

Ralph sighed. "It's a combination of hungry and angry. Like when you're so hungry you're cranky and snap at everyone."

Bram laughed. "Oh no, she's always like that."

Ralph took what was left on the tray and approached Gerontius and Torgrim, who were listening raptly to whatever Noel was lecturing on.

"We did have horses here, until the last century. But they have given way to the automobile." Noel was clearly in heaven, having an audience.

"You mean those objects of metal and glass we see through the window?" Torgrim asked, stroking his beard again. He took a carrot stick from the tray and chewed it thoughtfully. "They are pulled by invisible horses?"

"Not exactly," said Noel. "They move by themselves."

"What sorcery is this?" marveled Gerontius. "So many wonders!"

Ralph moved over to the bard, who was admiring Persephone's braid.

"It's called a fishtail braid," she was saying. "All my friends do it. We sometimes braid Cammi's hair when he lets us."

Cammi reddened. "Persephone!"

"What's wrong with that?" Persephone asked.

Mirak looked gently at Cammi. "Nothing at all, youngling. Why does this cause you such alarm?"

"It doesn't," said Cammi. "I guess it's not a big thing where you come from. But it sorta is here."

"Our people do not choose to wear our hair in such a fashion, but I can see how it would be quite becoming on you."

Then Mirak caught a glimpse of Ralph. Her eyes widened and she peered at his teeth. "But, young master! What horrible affliction has befallen you!"

Ralph looked at the others. "What are you talking about?"

Bram raised his hands to his mouth. "By the gods, I hadn't noticed. Who has cursed you thus?"

Noel came over and peered at Ralph and laughed. "RPG, I think they mean your braces."

Mirak looked with pity at Ralph and shook her head. "What manner of villain is torturing you thus, caging your teeth in bands of metal?"

Ralph rolled his eyes. "His name is Dr. Falatko, and he isn't torturing me. They're called braces, and they help to straighten my teeth."

"How barbaric!" declared Mirak. Catching a glare from Jandia, she added, "No offense."

Noel turned to Mirak. "People who have giant tusks growing out of their lower lips shouldn't throw stones, if you know what I mean."

Mirak's hand fell on her bow, and then she stopped herself.

"You should consider yourself lucky, youngling," said Gerontius. "Mirak takes the counsel of her human father's blood, rather than the brutal orc ways of her mother's race."

"That's one of the things I like about her," said Persephone, hugging the surprised bard.

"It is a struggle, but I reject my orc ways whenever I can, unless in battle."

"My parents have always taught me to respect the cultures of both their races," Noel said.

The five adventurers all looked confused.

"You're two races?" asked Bram.

"Yes. My mom is black, from Grenada, and my dad is white, from Boston," he said.

"White elf?" asked Jandia.

"Nope," said Noel. "They're both human."

"Then why do you say you are of two races?" asked Mirak. "I am of human and orc: two races. You are human and human."

"It's different for us," Jojo tried. "We're all humans, so—"

"So you are all of the same race!" said Torgrim impatiently.

"Well, yeah, we're all humans, but people see us differently," said Jojo. "Like, I'm white."

"And I'm Asian," added Persephone.

Ralph chimed in. "And I'm Jewish!"

"What does that have to do with anything?" Jojo asked.

Ralph reddened. "I dunno, but for some people it makes a difference."

"But you are human. And he is human. You are *all* human. I do not understand," said Jandia, shaking her head.

Cammi sighed. "Yeah, it's complicated."

"That's the most foolish thing I've ever heard," said Gerontius. "A human is a human. And a halfling is a halfling, and a dwarf is a dwarf." The wizard clapped his hands briskly. "But enough prattle," he added. "We must get down to business."

23

A MEETING OF MINDS

Gerontius turned his piercing gray eyes on Ralph. It was unnerving, as they seemed to have endless depths and yet to be so friendly at the same time.

"I am Gerontius Darksbane, wizard of the Forest Cloverdell. And this is—"

Noel was not going to wait for introductions when he had a chance to show off. "We know who you are. And that's Jandia Ravenhelm, barbarian warrior; Mirak Melodin, bard; the great cleric Torgrim Din-Mora; and Bram Quickfoot, rogue."

Gerontius regarded Noel for a moment. "We like to think of him as a scout, not a rogue."

"That is when I have not displeased them," said Bram as he took a fork and a knife from his pocket. Clearly Ralph was going to need to keep a close watch on the silverware.

"But how came you to know this?" asked Torgrim. "Have you a spell to look into our minds?"

"We know because we—" Jojo began before a sharp look from Ralph cut her off.

She realized that saying "we made you up" would probably be considered a rude and possibly dangerous thing to say to people with large swords and a giant war hammer.

"Go on," said Mirak.

Persephone piped up. "Because your fame is known far and wide. Even in our, um, dimension, or land or whatever, your history is known."

Jandia looked like she wasn't buying it. "How is this possible?"

Ralph decided to run with this. "We have heard tales," he added. "The stories of your search for the Seven Serpent Scepter has become a legend."

Bram gave a delighted laugh and grabbed an apple from the plate. "I told you we would be welcome here! You should trust me, Wizard!"

"The last time you said we would be welcomed, a giant bear with antlers and poisonous claws almost ripped my leg off," grumbled Jandia.

Bram shrugged and took a bite of his apple. "That was just his way of saying hello."

"But you have us at an advantage, younglings," Gerontius said. "We do not know what to call you."

Noel bowed. "Noel Carrington at your service."

Bram clapped. "Noel! What a fine name!"

"I am Persephone, named for the goddess of spring," exclaimed Persephone in her most "I have done many school plays" voice. She also read out loud in class with this voice, to the annoyance of everyone else.

"Your name matches you—it is as lovely as you are," said Mirak, making Persephone glow.

"My real name is Johnna, but everyone calls me Jojo," said Jojo simply.

Jandia placed a giant hand on her shoulder and looked her square in the face. "Johnna. It is a good name. A warrior's name."

Ralph winced when Gerontius turned to Cammi, who had pulled his baseball cap down onto his face. He hated to talk in class, and this was like ten times worse.

Gerontius knelt down and gently pulled Cammi's cap up. Cammi looked away.

"The others called you Cammi. Is this your given name?"

Cammi turned and looked at the elf's face. It seemed as though he'd never seen anything so beautiful in his life. A small shy smile snuck onto his lips. "My real name is Cameron," he said.

"That is a lovely name. But I prefer Cammi."

"So do I," Cammi said in the quietest voice possible.

Torgrim turned to Ralph. "And what, good lad, are you named?"

"I am named Ralph," he said.

There was a pause.

Then the entire group of adventurers burst out laughing.

"Ralph!" Bram said. "What kind of name is Ralph for a hero?"

Torgrim's entire belly was heaving up and down, he was laughing so hard. "Ralph? That's the name of the village idiot!"

"First of all, it's not cool to make fun of people with mental disabilities," Ralph said, trying to stop the ridicule. "And second of all . . . really? Making fun of people's names? Who's the kid here, anyway?"

Torgrim looked confused. "I wasn't making fun of anyone. That was Ralph's job in Barnsdale. He was the village idiot, and a very good one."

"Yes, you should be complimented!" said Bram with a smirk.

This was not going at all well. Ralph wanted to tell Torgrim that he initially had named the dwarf Fartnose the Great before Declan made him change it. See how he liked that.

"Deepest apologies, good young sir," said Mirak, wiping tears from her eyes. "That was inexcusably rude of us."

There was another pause.

"Ralph Ralph Ralph Ralph!" Jandia said, and they erupted in laughter all over again.

"He's not called Ralph," Jojo said. "We call him RPG."

"Oh! Much better," said Gerontius, completely unconvincingly.

"Whoo! I don't remember laughing that much in an age," said Torgrim, trying to catch his breath.

"So glad I could give you so much joy," Ralph said drily. "And I really hate to break up this lovely party, but we should be getting you back to your own world."

Gerontius looked confused. "But clearly we were summoned here."

"What do you mean?" asked Jojo.

Torgrim fingered the amulet around his neck. "It was the wizard who cast the spell to remove us from certain death, but he only cast the spell to send us to another place."

Mirak gestured around them. "Perhaps we are meant to be here."

Gerontius nodded. "I sense that someone has summoned us here. If not you, then what power has done this?"

24

A DECISION IS MADE

"The thing is, we kind of did summon you, I guess . . . ," said Noel. "Or at least, that did."

He gestured to the golden die. Now having completed its mission, it was silent and still, looking like nothing more than an average gold-colored metal die.

"We don't know that," Ralph said. "I mean, it could have been a coincidence."

Gerontius picked up the twenty-sided die and looked at it curiously. "I have seen the likes of this before. You, Halfling. You have gambled our very souls with such a trifle, have you not?"

He tossed the die to Bram, who caught it smartly in one hand. He held it up for the others to see. He peered at it, feeling the weight of it in his hand. "Yes, but mine is the simplest stone. In all my travels, this is my first time seeing one like this. I know gold, and this is solid and pure."

"Gold?" Torgrim's eyes lit up in spite of himself.

Ralph knew there was nothing dwarves in RoD liked more

than gold. They lusted after it and lost all reason in pursuit of it. "Don't get your hopes up. It was sent to me by a . . . stranger." He grabbed it out of the rogue's fingers.

"A stranger?" said Mirak. "So then we don't know where its powers are from."

"All I know is that something weird is going on," Ralph answered. "And the sooner we get you back to where you belong, the better it is for all of us."

"We are meant to be here," Torgrim muttered. "I know this is where we will find the last serpent."

Noel laughed. "If you guys want to find the Golden Serpent, you're not going to find it here."

Jandia let out a low growl and stepped forward menacingly. "How do you know of our quest?"

"Whoa, whoa!" said Jojo quickly, putting her hand on the barbarian's arm. "Chill out!"

Jandia placed her hand on the hilt of her sword. "She is casting a freezing spell! Cleric, protect me!"

Torgrim held his amulet up in front of him and his lips moved silently; then he swept his hand in the air in front of him.

Jandia jerked her head from side to side. "Your spell, Cleric. I see no glowing shield!"

"Perhaps in his excitement, he mixed up his words?" asked Bram.

"No Din-Mora in five hundred years has forgotten that spell," choked Torgrim. "Which means my magic does not work here."

Gerontius stepped forward and drew himself up to his full height. His slate-gray hair, pale face, and blazing eyes made for an impressive picture. "Adventurers, gather near me! We cannot stay here if we cannot protect ourselves!"

He held the orb aloft and chanted, *"Ozymanthus crysantius!"*

Cammi turned to Ralph and whispered, "That's the one to open a portal into another dimension."

There was an expectant hush. The orb came to life for a moment . . . then flickered and died.

The adventurers looked at one another, then at the children.

"Any other bright ideas?" asked Noel.

Ralph felt he had to say something. He was good at telling stories. All he had to do was do it now. "The tales of your quest to find the seven serpents are so famous, they have even reached our world."

Torgrim regarded Ralph for a long moment. "I do not think these children mean us any harm."

"No way!" Noel piped up. "We want to help!"

Jandia slowly lowered her sword.

Bram hopped to the window. "Young Noel, if our magic does not work here, we must find someone in this place who can help us." He turned to his fellow adventurers. "I say we move from this place."

Persephone turned to Ralph. "What time is it, anyway? I mean, they can't be here when our parents get back, right?"

Erk. Ralph hadn't even thought of that. "Yeah, you're right. We have a few more hours, at least."

Gerontius held up his hand. "We need more information about this world from these children."

Jandia leaned in. "Agreed." She turned to Jojo. "Tell us about this world. Is there truly no magic?"

"I don't think so," said Jojo, "but then again, I didn't think I'd be talking to a barbarian warrior with butter all over her face either. Come here." Jandia stepped back as Jojo reached out. "Your face is a mess. You really have to wipe it."

Bram smiled. "Clearly you have never taken a meal with a barbarian."

"We must be on one of the Astral Dominions," Mirak said. "Perhaps we should ascertain if it is good or evil?"

Gerontius turned to Cammi. "Good and gentle Cammi, you will speak the truth?"

"I'll try," Cammi said shyly.

Gerontius's eyes softened and he smiled. "Then I ask you, is this a place of good or evil?"

"I don't know." Cammi squirmed. "I mean, sometimes it's good and sometimes it's evil, I guess. Like most places."

"So this isn't one of the nine hells of Baator?" asked Torgrim.

"Nope, just one of the five boroughs of New York City," joked Noel. "Some people do think it's hell, but they're mostly tourists."

"So this is a city," said Bram as he helped himself to a glass of water.

"How big a city?" asked Gerontius. "Five thousand people?" Cammi shook his head. "Ten? Fifteen?" the Wizard continued.

"Um, a little more than that," mumbled Cammi.

"Oho!" said Mirak. "A great city indeed! I would wager fifty thousand at least!"

Bram laughed. "Let us say a hundred thousand, if you're going to make such a ridiculous claim."

"Actually, the current population of Brooklyn is about two and a half million people," Noel said helpfully.

"So this . . . Brooklyn . . . is no city," gasped Mirak. "It is an entire world."

"Well, to a lot of people here it kind of is," admitted Persephone.

Bram leapt to his feet and rubbed his hands. "Enough talk. I say we explore."

Jandia grunted. "I agree with the rogue. We are wasting time."

Ralph ran to the door. "Wait! You can't leave!"

"Why not?" Gerontius asked.

Ralph looked wildly at his friends for help.

"There are . . . enemies out there," Persephone said in her best scary-sounding voice.

Torgrim brandished his giant war hammer. "Even without spells, we can take care of ourselves."

Ralph pictured dozens of police cruisers descending on his street. "No, we cannot have anyone else see you."

Bram frowned. "But if we do not find the one with the magic to help us, we will be trapped here forever."

Gerontius turned to his fellow adventurers. "We need to find the last of the seven serpents. Once that is done, the power of the scepter shall return us to our world."

Jojo turned to Ralph. "Is that what the campaign said?"

"The campaign doesn't ever talk about the seventh serpent. Once you find it, you're supposed to make up that part of the story!"

"We'd better make up something fast," Noel said, "because they are definitely not staying."

Gerontius had pulled his silver sword from its sheath, and the others raised their weapons as well. "I warn you not to stand in our way. We will leave this house and seek our fate out there in this strange place."

The adventurers headed for the door.

25

WHAT SORCERY IS THIS?

Ralph looked on with dread as the adventurers reached the door. But then they stopped short, and Ralph and his friends watched as the group conferred in hushed voices (except Jandia, who seemed incapable of speaking in an indoor voice). "I am growing impatient!" she barked above the murmur of hushed voices. Finally, Gerontius drew himself up and turned to the kids.

"We have come to a decision. We need to learn more of this place. Venturing out by ourselves would be . . . unwise."

Of course.

All of a sudden, it dawned on Ralph that they would follow the rules of all RPGs. He needed to think of this as an adventure. And what was the first step after meeting the locals?

"You need a guide," Ralph said confidently. "And here you have five of them."

Mirak's face lit up. It was still somewhat unsettling to see her smile, with her large mouth and jutting lower fangs, but if you concentrated on the eyes, it was all right.

Persephone swept over to the door and ceremoniously offered Mirak her hand. "I will gladly be your companion on this journey!" she announced breathlessly, in her best "I am an actress" voice.

Gerontius held out his hand to Cammi, who shyly came forward. "Young master Cammi, would you teach me of your people?"

Jandia strode up to Jojo, grinned, and patted her on the back with her large pawlike hand. "You are with me!"

Jojo coughed and regained her balance. "All right!" she gasped.

Bram made a low, exaggerated bow to Noel. "Young Noel, I have a feeling we are kinsmen! Come and let us adventure together!"

Noel nodded delightedly and bowed back.

Ralph turned expectantly to Torgrim, who was glowering at him. "I guess I'm stuck with you, Ralph."

Ralph sighed. "The kids call me RPG, remember?"

"Oh, yes. But what means this . . . 'Arpy Gee'?" asked Torgrim, looking confused.

"They're the initials of my name," Ralph began, before deciding it was too long to explain.

"I'll just call ye Arpy, then," decided Torgrim, looking happier. "So, Arpy, have you a map to this town of millions, as you say?"

A map! Of course they would want a map. There was always a map in the games.

"We don't need a map. What we need is information," Noel said. "We know this neighborhood backward and forward."

"Are there any thieves and brigands about?" asked Bram.

"Are you kidding? This is Brooklyn!" said Noel, laughing. "That's why we have to be careful."

"Okay, before we go, I gotta text GG to let her know we're . . . uh, going for a walk." Ralph turned away for a second to tap on his phone.

When he returned to the group, he found the adventurers gathered, awestruck, around an embarrassed Jojo. She also had her phone out, open to the weather app, with a shining sun and drifting clouds on the screen.

"The magic glass! It calls up the very heavens!" whispered Torgrim.

"What sorcery is this?" demanded Gerontius.

"It's just a . . . Well, we use it to talk to people who are far away and get information," Persephone said.

"It is an enchanted box indeed," marveled Mirak.

"Take your finger and press there," Jojo said. "It can make music too."

"Perhaps this is a trap," Bram said.

Jojo shot him a look. "Gosh, you always think the worst of people. Just press it already, Mirak. Trust me."

Mirak tentatively reached out. "I do not need a spell?"

"If you end up getting captured inside that box, do not say you were not warned," said Jandia, who crossed her arms. "The wizard and cleric have no magic to protect you here."

Mirak locked eyes with Jojo and pressed the musical note icon. The screen changed and the music app opened. Mirak gasped with delight.

"Now push any of these," Jojo instructed. Mirak pressed.

The tinny speakers boomed out the bass line from the hit of the summer, and the drum kicked in a dance beat.

The adventurers nodded to the beat.

"It is a song of war!" Jandia said approvingly.

"Actually, it's a dance song," Cammi said.

"But it has drums!" Jandia pouted. "It is a war song. Maybe a dance of war song."

Jojo pressed the button to stop the song.

Mirak shook her head in amazement. "How incredible! You silence the magic with a touch of your finger."

Noel turned to Ralph. "So what's the plan?"

Ralph shrugged. "Just like in any game. We just need to go out there and hope to find someone or something that can help us."

Persephone had moved to the front and opened the door. A blast of hot early spring air greeted them.

"How is this possible?" asked Mirak. "It is cool and fresh inside the house, but fierce as the burning sun outside."

"What sorcery is this?" Gerontius said.

"There's a machine that takes the hot air and changes it into cool air inside the houses," Noel said helpfully. "Most people here have them."

"Truly remarkable," said Torgrim as he removed his helmet and wiped the sweat from his gleaming head.

The party headed out into the sunlight and proceeded down the steps of Ralph's stoop.

It was a late-April Saturday, and most of the families who lived on the block were either away for the weekend or enjoying the weather in the parks down by the piers. The quiet stillness was broken by the clanking of the swords, armor, and boots of visitors as they clumped down the stairs.

"I didn't realize they'd be so noisy," Cammi said to Persephone.

"I know. I don't think they'd be very good at sneaking up on people in real life."

Suddenly, a voice spoke in her ear. "Oh, I wouldn't be too sure about that." Persephone jumped and whirled around to see Bram, smiling that smirky smile of his.

"I forgot about you," she said. "You are a pretty good sneak, I guess."

"Comes in mighty handy, my girl," Bram said, "and it keeps people from talking about you behind your back."

Ralph saw that Jandia had strode ahead of the others, taking Jojo along down the block toward downtown Brooklyn. The rest of the party caught up just as they turned the corner, where there was the sound of hammers striking stone.

A crude voice called out, "Hey, guys! Get a load of her!"

26

AN ENCOUNTER WITH (TOO) FRIENDLY VILLAGERS

Ralph winced. He knew that voice. It belonged to one of the workmen on the street. Brooklyn Heights was a charming place filled with old brownstones, as the buildings were called (after the sandstone that was used to cover the bricks that made up most of the houses). Because the houses were all old, inevitably one or more of them were being restored at any time. The workmen on this particular house were big and burly and talked loudly, making nuisances of themselves, especially at lunchtime. Usually they were off on weekends, but sometimes the bosses brought them in on Saturdays to finish a job before the owners came back.

The man who spoke was wearing a sweat-stained sleeveless T-shirt and a yellow safety helmet. He was holding a hammer and a chisel. He was leering at Jandia.

He had two buddies. One had a bandana wrapped around his head and no shirt. His pink belly gleamed with sweat, and he was pushing a wheelbarrow filled with wet cement. The other had a baseball cap on backward and was wearing overalls. He held a trowel.

"Niiiiiiice!" Bandana said.

Jandia stopped. Gerontius held up his hand, keeping the rest of the party back from Jandia.

"This isn't going to end well," whispered Cammi to Gerontius.

"We shall see," answered the wizard with a small smile.

Overalls made kissing noises. Yellow Helmet put down his tools and cocked his head. "Smile, beautiful!"

Jandia coolly looked from man to man.

"Whatsamatter, honey? We're telling you you look good," said Overalls. He stood in her way.

"I would suggest you let the lady pass," Jojo said in the nicest way possible.

Yellow Helmet laughed. "I don't see no lady here. I see a chick in skintight shorts showing off everything she's got!"

"This is going to be good," said Torgrim.

Jojo smiled grimly and started backing away toward the others.

"And she's got a lot to show," said Overalls, guffawing as if it were the funniest thing anyone had ever said.

"Come on, sweetie. Don't you got anything to say? We're just being friendly." Yellow Helmet took a step toward the barbarian.

Ralph felt he had to do something before things got ugly. "Guys, I really wouldn't mess with her—"

Bandana answered Ralph without taking his eyes off Jandia, a nasty look on his face. "Nobody asked you, kid. Besides, we're just playin'. Right, boys?"

The others laughed, but it wasn't a good laugh. It was an ugly laugh. Filled with something gross and dirty.

It felt like it took less than a second.

Jandia picked up the man in the yellow helmet by the scruff of his neck like he was a puppy. She shook him and threw him into the wheelbarrow of cement. The gray muck splattered his two friends, who moved toward her. With a growl, she grabbed Bandana by the waistband of his jeans and the other man by the back straps of his overalls. She held them up for a moment, like two wriggling fish.

"I don't like the way you talk," she growled. She dropped them to the ground in a heap. They sat there, stunned, eyes wide.

Jandia turned to the others. "Should I let them live?"

"Yes, please!" said Ralph. "I don't think they'll give you any more trouble."

Yellow Helmet climbed out of the wheelbarrow. He was shaking.

"No more talking like that, do you understand?" Jandia hovered over the shaking Yellow Helmet.

"No, ma'am," he said in a little voice.

"We didn't mean no disrespect," said Overalls in an even smaller voice.

"I think you did," Jandia said. "I know your kind." She leaned in to the three cowering men. "If I hear of you not being nice to women, I will come back."

Bram came up and peered around Jandia. "Good gentlemen, if she does come back, I assure you she will cut off at least one part of your body. And I don't think she's decided which one yet."

There was a brief silence. And then the sound of clapping from across the street.

Ralph looked over and saw a nanny from one of the families from up the block with her stroller. There was also a young woman in colorful nurse's scrubs, and another with rainbow twists and a turquoise yoga mat. They were all applauding.

"You go, sister!" yelled the lady with the mat.

"They bother me every time I walk past!" added the nanny.

The nurse exchanged a high five with the nanny. "Me too! It's the last thing I need after a twelve-hour shift."

Jandia smiled as she watched the men clean themselves up.

She squared her shoulders. "All right. Now where?"

Ralph knew just the place. Where do campaigns always start?

BRAM AND THE COINS OF GOLD

Ralph called the kids together. "Look, every time we come to a new town in the game, where do we head?"

"A tavern!" said Cammi.

"So where's the nearest tavern?" asked Jojo. "I mean, it's not like we have them on every corner. . . ."

"Also, we're kids and can't go into one. Maybe we can find the modern equivalent? Like—"

"A coffee shop!" Ralph said, nodding. "My mom loves the Brooklyn Beanery. Let's try there."

They headed back to the adventurers, who were perched warily on a nearby stoop, looking around for more threats.

Gerontius looked up. "We are in your hands. We do desire food and drink. Is there a tavern nearby?"

"That's just what we were discussing," said Ralph. But food and drink? They'd just eaten half the food in his family's fridge. How hungry and thirsty were these people?

"Only one problem," Persephone said. "We don't have any money."

"I have three hundred dollars from my birthday!" Noel said. "But it's in the bank and I'm supposed to save it for college."

"Payment is not a concern, Arpy," Torgrim grunted. "Bram has a purse full of coin and I have a terrible thirst. So let us be off to this place."

Ralph turned to Bram. "About those coins . . ."

Bram pulled a small pouch attached to a cord around his neck. He opened it and proudly showed a handful of small round pieces of copper.

Gerontius raised an eyebrow. "I see concern in your faces. Surely there is enough there to get us what we need. The greediest taverner in all of Demos would not require that much for a simple meal."

Ralph stepped in. "I don't think they'll take your money. Copper is, well, not very valuable here."

Bram shrugged and put the coins back in his purse. "'Tis a pity. This is all we have in the world."

Noel laughed. "Well, sure. If you don't count that gold piece you stole from the mines of Ramgash and sewed into the seam of your vest."

Bram's eyes went as wide as saucers. "H-how could you have known that? What spell have you cast on me?"

Torgrim's face turned to an unpleasant shade of purple. "You WHAT?! Stole from a dwarven mine? I should pull those sharp little ears off your head, Rogue!"

Mirak stepped between the two smaller men, keeping them apart. "Explain yourself, Halfling. You have kept these from us?"

"I swear!" Bram protested, pointing at Noel. "He has put a spell on me! He put that coin in my vest!"

Ralph cocked his head at Noel. "In a way, he's right. You did steal that coin when we were in the mine."

"I was a rogue! What was I supposed to do?" Noel beamed. "I knew it would come in handy someday."

Cammi pulled on Gerontius's robe. "It doesn't matter how he got them. The important thing is that we can use gold."

The elven wizard knelt down and clapped Cammi on the shoulders. "The youngling speaks wisely, does he not? Arpy, is this indeed the coin of the realm?"

Great, thought Ralph. *Now everybody's calling me that.* "Yes, gold is very valuable here. We should be able to find a way of exchanging it."

Torgrim held out one of his large hairy hands. "Give me the coin, Rogue. And may the curse of Mora be upon you if you pull something like this again."

Bram carefully took the black-handled knife from its sheath and cut the threads on the lining of his vest. A gold piece tumbled out onto the dwarf's outstretched palm.

Ralph stared at the treasure. He had never seen anything like it in person. It reminded him of the chocolate coins wrapped in golden foil he would get at Chanukah, but this wasn't chocolate. At least, he hoped it wasn't.

"So where do we bring it?" asked Persephone in a worried voice. "A bank would ask too many questions."

"You think?" Noel smirked. "A bunch of kids trying to get money for a gold coin?"

"Robinov's!" Ralph exclaimed. He was greeted with blank faces. "You know," he said, "that jewelry store right off Court Street!"

Jojo made a face. "That dusty old place? Is it still in business?"

"I thought it closed years ago," said Noel.

"No, it's still there," insisted Ralph. "My dad always looks in the window when we go by. He likes the vintage watches."

They had reached the corner. The traffic light was against them, and cars were streaming across the intersection.

Gerontius stroked his chin and observed. "It seems we have reached a puzzle. How to get across this path? They will not stop."

Mirak indicated the red hand on the sign under the light. "The hand prevents us from safe passage."

"Perhaps we need to climb the pole and leap over," said Bram, who had already hopped up to the light pole.

"No!" yelled Ralph. "Just wait."

There was a pause.

"Why do we wait?" asked Torgrim with impatience. "They will not stop."

"We wait for the light to change," explained Cammi.

The adventurers looked around, confused.

"We must wait for the sun to lower in the sky—is that what you mean?" said Mirak.

"No! Just the little light—you see?" said Jojo, pointing to the red light.

Sensing that the light was about the change, Noel decided to have a little fun. He held up his hands. "Oh merciful gods of traffic, allow us to pass!" he intoned.

To the astonishment of the adventurers, the light changed to green, the red hand turned into a white image of a walking man, and the cars stopped.

The five travelers nodded to one another.

"He has great power," Bram whispered to Torgrim.

"So I see," said Torgrim. "We have much to learn from this young mage."

Ralph and the others ushered them across the street.

This was Court Street, the hub of downtown Brooklyn. Unlike on the side streets, there were plenty of people here.

"You know, I thought they would be getting a lot more attention," said Jojo.

"Are you kidding?" Persephone rolled her eyes, gesturing around her. "This is Brooklyn. Look at these people."

She had a point. Across the street, there was a skinny man in black leather shorts with no shirt and multiple tattoos. Passing him was a young girl with bright pink hair, pushing a stroller with a ferret in it.

"I guess you're right." Jojo shrugged as they walked up to the dusty window of the old jewelry shop.

28

THE RING OF TRUTH

Downtown Brooklyn had changed throughout the years, and not always for the better. Up until the seventies, it had been filled with local bookstores, family-owned bakeries, and butcher shops. Then came the bad times during the economic downturn in the 1980s, when no one would shop there, when the area was filled with disreputable bargain stores and even a betting parlor where sad little men lost their meager pension money on horse races. Some of the older shops held on by their fingernails, waiting for the times to change.

But when they did, the businesses that came in were gleaming cell phone stores, drugstore chains, and places selling high-priced running shoes. The rents had simply gotten too high for the mom-and-pop stores to last.

True, there was still the occasional old-school pizzeria or fast-food store that catered to office workers on their lunch hours. Otherwise, Robinov's was a legacy of that earlier time. Who knew how it had managed to stay put? Perhaps Mr.

Robinov had had the foresight decades ago to buy the property. Or maybe he had signed a lease of a hundred years, on the chance that his children would take over the store when he retired.

It certainly didn't look like anyone had changed the sign since it had opened. ROBINOV'S FINE JEWELRY FOR ALL OCCASIONS, it said in neon script behind a window that hadn't been cleaned since its opening. Past all the dust and grime, boxes and boxes of old watches were partially visible, stacked haphazardly. Not really a display so much as a hoard.

Bram's eyes brightened at the sight of so many shiny baubles. "Look, Gerontius! They seem to be tiny clocks! Small enough to wear!"

Gerontius nodded. It appeared to Ralph that the wizard had long since given up trying to make sense of this strange new world and was just taking it in, processing it as best he could. Or perhaps there was a plan forming in that mysterious elven head. Even in the game, when Cammi played him, Gerontius was something of a cipher. Cammi didn't always let on everything he was thinking to the others, loving secrets as much as he did.

Ralph turned to Torgrim. "You and I should probably go in. I don't think there's room for all of us."

"Wise words, Arpy," Mirak said. "Shall we meet at the tavern?"

Persephone turned to Ralph. "That might not be a bad idea. It's just up the block, and it's awfully hot out here." She looked over at the others, clad in leather and heavy cloth. "Especially for them."

"Good plan. We'll meet you there," said Ralph.

Persephone led the others away, toward the blue sign of the Beanery, the local coffee shop chain.

Ralph pushed open the door to the jewelry store. To his dismay, it wasn't air-conditioned. Torgrim came in behind him, clanking in his chain mail. An old-fashioned fan wheezed on top of the glass counter. The inside of the tiny shop was just as inviting as the outside, dusty and cramped, with boxes everywhere. There were posters clinging to the wall with yellowed tape, proclaiming names like Waltham and Tissot.

Other than the coughing fan, there was no noise in the shop. It was as if time had stopped, and not just on the faces of so many unwound watches.

Ralph gazed down into another glass case, where diamond rings were neatly lined up in velvet boxes. Torgrim leaned in, his eyes locked on the treasure. If a dwarf loves anything more than gold, it is precious jewels.

"Perhaps . . . we can trade this gold for . . ." Torgrim gestured hopefully.

Ralph shook his head. "We're not here for that. Your belly is empty and you're thinking of diamonds."

Torgrim sighed. "Your words are true, young Arpy Gee. But even in this dark dungeon of a shop, see how they shine!"

A voice called from the back. "Someone there? Listen, I have a gun. Don't do anything stupid."

"We're customers!" Ralph called back.

"That's different!" the voice said. There was a groan as if someone were raising themselves from a chair with great difficulty. Then a shuffling noise, and finally a head appeared around the doorway.

It occurred to Ralph that if he didn't know any better,

he might have thought Mr. Robinov was Torgrim's long lost cousin. About the same size, with a broad chest under a dirty white apron, he had a thick white beard and small glasses perched on his bulbous nose. He peered at the two of them on the other side of the counter.

"Yes? So what is it you want? Watches? I have watches. Rings? A nice necklace, perhaps?"

"No thank you," said Ralph. "We're here to sell you something."

Mr. Robinov's expression changed to one of disgust. "Not interested."

"But—" Ralph protested.

The old man gestured around him. "Does it look like I need to buy anything? I have enough stock as it is. Thanks, but no thanks."

Torgrim cleared his throat. "You have an impressive stock, Jeweler, but surely you will buy something of value."

"What? An old ring? I got plenty of old rings. A vintage watch? I got hundreds of 'em. I tell you, I'm not interested."

Torgrim held out his closed hand. "You haven't one of these, I warrant." He opened it to reveal the gleaming gold coin within.

Robinov stopped and leaned in. He shrugged. "All right, I'm interested. Is it solid gold?"

Torgrim bristled. "Do you dare to question the work of my people?"

Robinov looked at Ralph. "Just asking a simple question. No need to get so touchy."

"He's a little sensitive about that kind of thing," Ralph said, taking the coin from Torgrim, who was muttering a curse of some kind under his breath. He handed the coin to Robinov, who took a jeweler's loupe and peered at the object with fascination.

"Never seen one like this before," murmured the old man. "May I ask where you got it?"

"It was taken from the mines of Ramgash and coined by the dwarves of the Western Woods," Torgrim said in a hushed voice.

Robinov stared at him for a moment. "Yeah, okay. Whatever. I just need to know where you got it. I mean, I don't take stolen goods, you understand."

"Stolen! These have been in the Din-Mora family for a thousand years! Dwarven blood has been spilled protecting them from the dragons of the Black Skies!" bellowed Torgrim indignantly.

"No need to shout," said Robinov. "I have to ask." He turned to Ralph. "So what do I write down on the form? If it's real gold, I have to say something."

Ralph sighed. "Just say it's a family heirloom."

"Okay, now we're getting somewhere," said Robinov. "Let's see what we have."

He reached under the counter and brought out a small vial. He was about to open it when he paused. "You know, I was going to do the acid test, but I think this calls for something else."

"There is one true test, the only way to truly judge if gold is pure," said Torgrim.

Robinov smiled. It was the first time Ralph had seen him look happy. He seemed to recognize a soul mate in the cleric. "Yes, of course. The ring of truth."

"That is it precisely," said Torgrim, who nodded.

"Young man, perhaps you've heard that expression. Well, this is where it comes from. Listen closely. Perhaps you'll learn something today," said Robinov to Ralph as he reached under the counter once more and pulled out a small wooden box. It was beautifully made, and the surface was rubbed smooth, as if it had been stroked and loved by generations of Robinovs.

The jeweler pulled something out of his pocket. It appeared to be another gold coin.

"You see this?" he asked Ralph. "Is it gold or only gold-plated?"

Ralph inspected the coin. It looked real. It felt heavy in his hand. "It could be real, I guess."

Torgrim grinned. "It could be, at that. Or just base metal plated with a covering of gold, enough to fool a stupid merchant."

Robinov bowed to Torgrim. "Your friend here is quite an expert. Nice beard, by the way."

Torgrim smoothed his braided beard. "Where I come from, men are proud of their beards and treat them with respect."

"You were showing me something," Ralph persisted.

"Yes, of course. Well, let's see." Robinov opened the wooden box. A small trove of gold coins could be seen inside. He selected one. "Here. If I hold the coin in question between my fingers like so and strike it with the genuine gold coin, let us see what happens."

He held the coin from his pocket between his thumb and forefinger and hit it with the gold coin from the box. A dull *thunk* could be heard.

Robinov looked over his glasses at Ralph. "That's gold plate. Dull. Nothing. Maybe worth twenty bucks. Now let's see your coin."

Gently, he picked up the dwarven-mined coin. A ray of sunlight passed through the dusty window and gleamed off the coin as the jeweler held it aloft. He paused for a moment, and then struck it with the other coin.

There was an unmistakable peal, a ringing, reverberating sound. It lasted a good ten seconds, getting deeper and then slowly fading away in the silence of the shop.

"The ring of truth," Robinov said quietly. He met Torgrim's gaze and bowed his head.

"Forgive me for doubting you, sir." His tone had changed.

"The world is full of cheats and liars," Torgrim replied. "You have met your fair share, I would not doubt."

"You can say that again, fella," Robinov said. He took out a scale and carefully balanced the counterweights on one side and the coin on the other. He let out a low whistle.

"One ounce of pure gold." He turned to Torgrim. "The market is up today. You're lucky. I can give you a thousand dollars in cash for it."

Torgrim looked at Ralph. "Arpy, is this a good price?"

"Y-yes! This is a very good price!" Ralph stammered.

The old man shuffled off to the back office to get the money from his safe. He returned with an envelope. "Count it. I only have hundreds."

Ralph opened the envelope and almost dropped it. He carefully counted out ten one-hundred-dollar bills. That would be plenty of money for now.

Robinov reached out and shook Torgrim's hand. "A pleasure

doing business with you. If you ever want to sell some more, you know where to come."

"Excellent, my good man. You are an honorable jeweler and shall have our custom if ever we are in need again," Torgrim said.

He and Ralph headed out onto the sunny Brooklyn sidewalk. Ralph turned to look at the dusty, decrepit store once more. "If we do, I hope he's still here."

Robinov clearly had overheard him. "Of course I'll be here! I'll always be here!" he called, laughing. "Where else would I go?"

29

THE GAME OF CUPS

Cammi gingerly pushed open the door to the Brooklyn Beanery and gestured for the others to come in. "There's some space in the back," he said, threading his way through the tables filled with earnest young people. They found a table and sat down. Almost no one looked up from their work, or whatever they were engrossed in.

"Now what?" asked Jojo.

Bram scanned the room with a practiced eye. "We need money, that is certain. And why wait for that grumbler of a dwarf and your friend, who seems a wee bit boring, if I may say so."

"RPG's not boring," Persephone protested. "He just . . . likes to do things the right way."

"Well now, what's the fun in that?" Bram asked, looking around. "We can get plenty of money right here." He spied what he was looking for, and somehow, without anyone even noticing, he leapt from his chair and retrieved three coffee mugs and a paper napkin from behind the bar. He reached back and wet the napkin with a bit of water and wadded it up. "This should do nicely." He squeezed it between his hands, making a small ball.

The halfling looked from one of the kids to the next. "Now, you really haven't any money?" he asked.

Noel reached into his pocket. "Well, I do have five dollars. But it's my allowance, and it's not enough to buy stuff for everyone."

Jandia looked confused. "But that is paper. How is that used to acquire what you need?"

"Look, it's kind of hard to explain our monetary system right now," Noel said with a sigh. "Just understand that we use both coins and paper. The five on the paper tells the merchant its worth."

Jandia snorted. "If you say so. So we should just take some paper and write numbers on it!"

"Forget it," said Noel. "We also use coins, if that makes more sense to you."

Bram's face lit up. "Coins! Anyone have any coins?"

Jojo dug into her warm-up jacket and came up with a pair of quarters. "This is all I have."

Bram examined the coins with great curiosity. "Why, aren't they lovely! And these are worth more than that paper, I assume?"

Noel put his palm up to his face. "You explain, Persephone."

"Actually, you would need twenty of these to make one of these," she explained, "as four of these coins make one dollar and this is a five-dollar bill."

"I've got it now!" said Bram. "We're all set."

"Set for what?" asked Cammi nervously.

"Oh, let him do what he will," said Jandia sourly. "He'll do it anyway, so you might as well save your breath."

"All I need is someone to be my little helper," Bram said with a grin.

Noel leapt out of his chair like he did in class. "Me! Me!"

Bram gently pushed him down. "No, Noel, my lad. I think not. You've an honest face. And a tongue to match." His eyes settled on Persephone. "Now, Miss Likes to Pretend, I think you're the one for this job."

Persephone glanced at the others. "Me? But I'm no liar."

"It's not exactly lying, lassie," said Bram. "More like a performance."

Persephone immediately perked up. "That's different! Who do I play?"

Bram rubbed his hands together. "You'll see! Now come sit by me and I'll explain!" Persephone scampered over and Bram whispered in her ear. She listened for a moment, giggled, and then nodded. "I can do that!"

Cammi turned to Gerontius to see what he made of all this. He found the wizard staring in fascination at the other tables. At last he turned to Cammi.

"These poor people. Who has enchanted them in this way?"

Cammi looked at the people. They seemed like a pretty normal Brooklyn crowd: all different races, ages, and cultures jammed up together, doing their best to get along. Not particularly enchanting.

"In what way?" he asked.

"Each is transfixed, staring into their magic mirrors. I have watched, and except for wiggling their fingers on the little buttons in front of them, none has moved."

Cammi looked and saw table after table of people on their laptops. It was kind of creepy, now that he thought about it.

"I have figured out that they are being guided by some spirit who speaks to them through those devices clamped to their ears," Gerontius said, indicating the headphones each was wearing.

Cammi was going to explain what really was going on and then decided it was simply too complicated. "Yes, you're right. That's exactly what's going on," he said simply.

Gerontius smiled and nodded. "I am figuring out your world at last!"

There was a commotion in the corner. A group of people had gathered around a table. Bram had the small ball of paper, and he was passing it between the three cups, which were turned over onto the table. "Can you guess which one it's under? It takes the eye of an archer and the quickness of a hawk!"

A bunch of tourists were watching the hypnotic movement as the ball passed.

Bram looked up. "How about you, young lady?"

Persephone looked at her friends. She giggled and pointed at the middle cup.

Bram raised it. The paper ball was there. "Bravo! Good for you, miss! Anyone else?"

He moved the balls around again, and one of the tourists jokingly pointed to the one on the right. It also had the ball.

Bram shook his head, amazed. "Why bless me! I've come to the wrong place if I thought I could fool you good people."

Persephone was whispering with Jojo and Noel. She turned around. "I bet I can do it again."

"Can you, now? I'm not so sure of that, little one."

Persephone held out the two quarters. "I bet I can."

Bram cocked his head. "Now you make it interesting. I am so confident that I can fool you, I will put up one of these against your coins," he said, putting down the five-dollar bill.

Now the tourists were definitely interested.

Bram moved the cups around again. This time, it seemed as if they were moving faster, but if you kept your eye on the cup with the ball, it was clear it was the one on the left this time. Persephone hesitated. She began to point to the center cup, but one of the tourists, a lady in hot-pink shorts and a straw hat, called out to her. "Honey, it's the one on the left!"

Bram looked annoyed. "It is her choice to make. Unless you are playing, please refrain from prattling on."

Persephone looked innocently at the woman, who nodded so hard it looked like her head might dislodge.

"If you're sure . . . ," Persephone said, and pointed to the one on the left.

And there it was. The tourists cheered, and Bram glared at them as he handed the money over to Persephone.

"This is awesome!" she squealed.

"My turn!" said the woman in the pink shorts. She took out her money.

WHAT'S LOVE GOT TO DO WITH IT?

As the tourists and other patrons gathered around to play Bram's game, Persephone and Jojo walked away.

"I do hope he knows what he's doing," Persephone said.

Jandia looked bored. "He is very skilled. He will let them win a few times, to make it look honest. They will think it a merry sport. Bram is a liar and a cheat. Thank the gods."

Noel's face was glowing as he turned around. "He's so good! I have to figure out how he does this! Maybe he'll teach me!"

Persephone took her five dollars and went to the counter. The barista was a slim young man with his hair tied up in a bun on top of his head. He had a day's growth of beard and bright blue eyes. The tag on his shirt said DASHIELL.

"What can I get you, sweetheart?" he asked.

"A small latte, please, um, Dashiell," Persephone said, blushing a little.

"You can call me Dash," the young man said, and took out a pen. "Your name?"

"It's Persephone, um, Dash. Spelled *P-E—*" Persephone began.

"I know." Dash smiled. "Like the goddess."

Persephone watched his bicep flex as he wrote her name on the cup. She hoped he didn't notice.

"Speaking of goddesses," Dash said, "didn't you come in with that woman over there?" He pointed to Jandia, who was glaring fiercely at no one in particular.

Persephone slumped. Of course. "Yeah. She's . . . a friend of my brother's."

"Cool," Dash said. "Hey, you can sit down. I'll bring your latte."

Persephone slouched over to where Jandia was sitting and plopped down next to her and Jojo. "The barista likes Jandia," she reported to Jojo.

"Dash? The hot one? No way!" Jojo exclaimed.

"Yes way," Persephone said. "You'll see when he comes over."

"He's not coming over," Jojo said. "He always makes you get your own drink."

"Here you go!" said a cheerful voice, and Dash placed Persephone's latte in front of her as she looked victoriously over at Jojo.

"And I brought an espresso for your friend," he said, placing a small cup of the thick strong Italian coffee in front of Jandia, who barely acknowledged it. He took a seat next to her.

"I really like your ink," he said, pointing to the tattoos on her arms. He held up his own, which had a generous amount of artwork on them. "Where did you get yours done?"

Jandia turned and faced him. He gave her a dazzling smile, which was not returned.

"They were given to me by the priests in my village," she said simply.

"The village?" Dash said. "I got mine done there too! On Saint Mark's Place."

"Not Greenwich Village," Jojo quickly explained. "She meant the village where she comes from."

"Oh, cool! I thought I heard an accent!" Dash said with practiced charm, which was not working in the slightest, sadly. "So where are you from?"

"The mountains of Warthog. How I wish I were back there right this moment."

"I know about that. I'm from Nebraska, and sometimes I just want to chuck it all and go home too. But I've got a band, and I couldn't just let them down like that. You should come hear us play. We play this kind of fusion of bluegrass and death metal. . . ." His voice trailed off as Jandia opened her mouth and gave a gigantic yawn.

Jojo listened to this with amazement. He certainly was persistent.

Dash tried another tack. "So . . . do they have any significance? Your tattoos, I mean. I was told these were Celtic ceremonial bands," he said, pointing to his own arm, "but you never know about these things." He touched Jandia on the arm where her tattoos were.

Jandia shifted in her seat, pulled her arm away, and looked Dash full in the face. "I won them. Each ring represents a man I killed in battle. Their blood was mixed with the ashes of their bones, and the priests used the swords of my defeated enemies to cut these marks deep in my flesh. This is why I fear no man."

Dash nodded, his face turning an interesting shade of white. "Right. Okaaay. So, that's cool. Listen, I have to get back to the bar. I think I have some customers waiting."

He backed away.

Persephone shook her head. "That was cold, for sure."

"I would not have talked to him thus," Mirak agreed, "but Jandia is who she is." Under Jandia's icy glare, the two moved down the table.

Jojo poked Jandia in the arm.

"What is it, girl?" snapped the barbarian.

"You didn't have to be so rude to him," Jojo said. "He's cute."

"He was forward and too familiar," Jandia said. She thought for a second. "What do you mean by this, *cute*? In our world, *cute* is a word for children."

Jojo looked away. "I mean he was kind of hot—you know, good-looking."

"And this is important to me?" Jandia laughed.

Jojo turned and faced Jandia. "Well, you know, I mean . . . don't you like that? When a guy flirts with you?"

"Again, you are using words that confuse me," Jandia said.

Jojo tried again. "Okay, in your world. Has there ever been a man you wanted to, you know . . . kiss? Or who you find yourself thinking about all the time?"

Jandia smiled. "Ah! Now I see! You mean mating!"

Jojo turned bright red. "No! Well, not just that."

"Yes, you mean mating," Jandia insisted. "A man and a woman decide to mate, and then—"

Jojo stopped her. "Yes, I know. I take health class. I'm talking about love. That's different."

Jandia looked over where Mirak and Persephone were deep in conversation. "I think I know now what you mean. The bard sings stories of the gods who fall in love. Or princes and princesses. Always talking about the moon or stars or being together for all time."

"Yes, like that," Jojo said.

"We are warriors. Warriors are bred to fight." Jandia grabbed the hilt of her sword. "This is my companion. All I need is this and a good horse. A man is for breeding, I suppose, when I am older and cannot kill them."

"That's a very sad attitude," Jojo said.

Jandia peered at Jojo for a moment. "Ah. So, you? You have someone you wish to mate with?"

"No!" Jojo almost screamed. "It's not like that. I mean, I do have a crush. Do you know what it means to have a crush on someone?"

"Of course," said Jandia. "I have crushed many men. Sometimes the skull, sometimes just an arm or a leg . . ."

"Not that kind of crush. It's like what I was saying before. It's like a feeling you get when you see them. All kind of weird inside. You can't stop thinking about them. They're special."

"And you feel this way about someone?"

Jojo looked down. "Yeah, I guess I do."

Jandia's face lit up. "It is RPG, yes?"

"Are . . . are you kidding?" Jojo stammered. "Him? Not in a million years. No way."

Jandia shrugged. "Why not? He is cute, as you say. Like a little bunny."

"Exactly." Jojo nodded. "Like a little bunny. No, the boy I like is named Jared. He's on the soccer team, and he's really funny and smart. . . ."

Jandia rolled her eyes. "You sound like the women in the court of my kingdom. Simpering little wretches. You are better than that. You could be a warrior. Do not waste your thinking time on boys."

"But it's nice," insisted Jojo. "You can be a warrior and like someone. Take, I don't know . . . Gerontius. He is very good-looking, don't you think?"

Jandia regarded Gerontius.

"He is very pale," she said. "But he is certainly very pretty."

"So?" asked Jojo, grinning.

Jandia paused. "I do not think he likes our kind."

Jojo smiled. "I see. You mean he will only, um . . . be . . . with elvenborn. I get it."

Jandia coughed. "No, that is not what I meant. I mean . . . our kind. He has spoken often of a boy whom he was very close to in his growing up. They were, he said, special friends."

Jojo swallowed. "Okay. Now I see what you mean."

"It is a very sad story," Jandia continued. "They were much like the people in Mirak's songs, so he says. I do not know the rest."

"I do," said Mirak, who had come and joined them.

"They were deeply together. But the elves of his forest were not happy with this, and the elders took it upon themselves to split them apart."

"That's not right," Jojo said, "but we have people like that here as well."

"They put a spell on his beloved, and the poor boy took sick," Mirak continued. "No matter what Gerontius did, he could only watch as the lad wasted away. He was helpless."

Jojo looked over at Gerontius, who was in conversation with Cammi.

"From the day his friend passed over into the realm of darkness, he has devoted himself to his studies. He soon became more powerful than any of the wizards in his forest. That is why they banished him from his people."

Jojo sighed.

Then she looked through the window of the coffeehouse and saw exactly what she did not want to see. A police car had stopped outside, and an officer was heading directly toward them.

OBERON WANTS HIS FOCACCIA

Jojo clutched Persephone's arm. "Do you—"

Persephone had her eyes glued to the door. "Yes, I see. This isn't good."

"I'm pretty sure having a six-foot sword isn't legal in New York City," Cammi said.

"Why are you fearful, little ones?" asked Mirak.

"Um . . . they're kind of like magistrates," Jojo tried. "We call them the police."

Mirak and Jandia froze. Gerontius's hand was on the hilt of his sword.

The officer opened the door a crack and peered into the coffeehouse. His eyes almost found them, but at the last second they rested on the menu by the window. He let out a low whistle.

"Jeez! Four bucks for a small coffee!" he said to no one in particular. He turned back to yell to the driver of the patrol car. "Hey, Sarge! This place is a rip-off! Let's just go to the deli on the next block."

"You got it!" the driver yelled back. The officer pulled his head out of the doorway, jumped into the car, and drove off.

"That was close," said Cammi.

"I think we could have handled them, young friend," said Gerontius gently. "But we appreciate your concern."

"What did we miss?" said Bram, swaggering over to the table. In his hand was a wad of bills.

"It was amazing!" Noel said to the others. "They didn't suspect a thing!"

Bram sat down and waved to the tourists, who waved back. "I'll get you tomorrow!" the husband of the woman in the pink shorts called out. He was wearing an I ♥ NY T-shirt.

"I'll be here waiting!" Bram answered cheerfully.

"We're coming back tomorrow?" asked Noel, confused.

"Of course not," Persephone said. "He just said that to make them feel like they'd have a chance to win their money back."

Bram looked at her with admiration. "Persephone, my sweet, you have the makings of a fine rogue."

"Thanks, I guess," she said.

Jandia grunted and pointed at the door, where Ralph and Torgrim had appeared. "You certainly took your time," she called.

"We saw the police car and waited to see what was going to happen," Ralph said.

"You mean you were waiting to let us fight your battle, Dwarf," Jandia said.

"No one has ever fought my battles, Barbarian. You better than anyone know that," Torgrim spat. "Did I not save your mangy hide at the Battle of Weston Falls?"

"I think we better get these guys something to eat before a fight breaks out," Ralph whispered to Jojo. He turned to the others. "There's a little grocery store next door. Let's go get some food."

"We can save what money you got for the coin," Noel said, "since Bram won sixty bucks off those tourists."

"But . . . but . . . that's . . ." Ralph tried to find a word other than *illegal.*

Noel shrugged. "What can you do. Rogues, am I right?"

They followed the others out the door.

Dash watched in fascination as they left. "Why do I always pick the crazy ones?" he asked his coworker.

The grocery store wasn't much better than the coffee shop. Torgrim looked like he was about to cry when he found out there was no mutton. Just as the adventurers started to understand the concept of putting meat and cheese between pieces of bread, Noel suggested they just get a deli platter and bring it back to Ralph's. This seemed to make the most sense, and all was going well until the adults tried to buy bottles of Brooklyn craft ale (thank goodness Brooklyn had become so hip that drinking ale had become quite fashionable again).

"ID, please," said the bored cashier to Jandia and Mirak. This was not good.

"I beg your pardon, good lady?" asked Mirak in her most charming voice.

"I need some identification."

"I can certainly identify myself," said Mirak. "I am Mirak, daughter of Kraagina and Prince Stephan Hightower, lately high bard to the court of King Andromodus."

The cashier stared impassively at her.

"Nice titles. They go well with the teeth. I still need to see ID."

Ralph tugged at Mirak's sleeve. "It's a law here. You need to be at least twenty-one years old to buy spirits."

"That's not a problem," grumbled Torgrim. "I'm a hundred and four! That's plenty old enough, I should think."

"It's not just that. You need a card that proves it," Noel added helpfully.

"Why? Can a twenty-one-year-old grow a beard like this?"

The guy cutting the deli meat glanced over. "I don't know, I went to school with a kid who could grow a beard like that in ninth grade."

By this time, a crowd was gathering behind them. People wanted to order their lunches.

"Hey, what's the holdup, Rosa?" asked a man in a Yankees cap.

"Look, do you have ID or not? Otherwise, pay for the platter and that's it." Rosa was clearly getting impatient.

"This is ridiculous!" chimed in a woman with a toddler who was clearly about to melt down. "Oberon, darling," she cooed to him, "Mommy is getting your focaccia."

Persephone dragged Gerontius to the front of the group. She looked up at Rosa with wide eyes. "I'm so sorry we're holding things up. Dad, show her your ID."

Gerontius looked at Persephone like she had two heads. Or possibly three.

"Yes, well, my . . . daughter . . . that seems to be an issue. . . ."

"I want my focaccia now!" screamed little Oberon.

"Of course, my darling," cooed his mother. Turning to Rosa, she hissed, "Can't you speed things up a little, please!"

Persephone looked at Gerontius and shook her head. "Dad!

Don't tell me you left your wallet in our apartment again!" She turned to Rosa. "He does this all the time."

"Open another cash register!" someone shouted from the end of the line.

"Sofia called in sick today! I'm the only cashier!" yelled the frazzled Rosa as the platter was deposited in front of her. She looked at Gerontius's gray hair and then at his ice-gray eyes, which met hers with such power that she lost her breath.

"Well . . . I guess . . . if you left it in your apartment . . . ," she stammered.

"Of course it is in my apartment, as she said," replied the wizard. "And we don't want to keep these good people waiting, do we?"

"FOCAAAACCIIIAAA!" came a wail from the floor.

"What is an 'apartment,' by the way?" whispered Gerontius out of the corner of his mouth.

"I'll tell you later!" hissed Persephone.

By now the sound from the floor had devolved into a siren-like screech.

"I haven't heard anything like that since the screaming worms of the caverns of Kryll," said Torgrim, holding his ears. "What is this fohkasheeyah that he finds so valuable?"

Noel looked smug. "It's a type of Italian bread."

"That's twenty-five for the platter and another twenty for the two six-packs of ale," the cashier said quickly, ringing them up.

Persephone handed her the cash. "Next time, Dad, remember your wallet!" she admonished Gerontius, who smiled at the cashier as Jandia and Mirak grabbed their provisions.

Bram shook his head. "A rogue in the making, I tell you. She's a natural!"

Exiting the store, Ralph led them down a quieter side street. He couldn't handle any more of the adventurers' attention-getting.

Torgrim pulled at Noel's sleeve. "So, what news did you hear in the tavern?"

Noel sighed. "We didn't."

"It was a room of bewitchment," murmured Gerontius. "The patrons were enchanted, staring at those magic screens, cut off from the world. Very troubling. Perhaps a curse of some kind."

"My parents would agree," said Jojo. "I'm only allowed to use mine for homework and on the weekends."

"You mean they do that voluntarily?" asked Mirak.

"Not everyone is doing that," protested Noel. "A lot of people are outside too."

"Ah, I see." Gerontius nodded. "They have smaller ones they carry with them instead."

He gestured to the people passing them. It certainly did seem as though everyone was staring down at their phones instead of talking to one another.

"Perhaps it is how their rulers control them," Torgrim said, stroking his beard. "They give them visions that keep them amused and docile."

Ralph thought about this for a moment. "Maybe you're right. But we don't see it that way."

"Of course you don't," said Bram. "The enchanted ones never do! That is the beauty of it! The pig in the trough has no idea what's in store for him either! He simply eats and rolls in the mud!"

The kids looked at one another.

"Wow. That's kind of a creepy way to look at it," said Cammi.

"I do watch a lot of videos," admitted Noel. "But I learn a lot too."

"You can learn more from living life itself, I warrant," said Gerontius.

"Your knowledge comes from books!" protested Ralph.

"That is true. And there is also a danger to living one's life with one's head in a book," admitted Gerontius with a small smile.

"We do need knowledge, though," said Mirak. "And I fear we will not find it on your magic screen, or even in the wizard's magic book."

They waited at the corner. The light turned green.

"That is the spell for the vehicles to stop and let us pass." Gerontius nodded confidently. He started to cross the street, followed by the others. "I am starting to learn the ways of this world," he said to himself.

"Wizard!" Jandia called out, motioning in the direction of the street to their left. "Perhaps here is where we find knowledge!"

SPARE CHANGE

They all looked in the direction she was pointing. A gaunt homeless man stood there holding a sign with PLEASE HELP scrawled on it.

"Aha!" said Bram with delight. "A beggar! We shall certainly get something from him!"

"I don't think that's such a good idea," said Ralph.

"Why not?" asked Mirak. "We always ask beggars for information. Sometimes you cross their palms with silver, or else—"

"I know," said Ralph impatiently. Anyone who had played Reign of Dragons more than a few times knew that at some point in every adventure a beggar would come along at exactly the right time and either give you the precise information you needed, or else make some prophecy that sounded odd, but once you figured it out, it provided the answer you were looking for.

"It's just that beggars . . . Well, we don't really call them

that. We call them homeless people, usually," said Persephone.

"But he's asking for money," said Noel, logical as always,
"so isn't he begging?"

"He's asking for money," said Jojo, "but that's ... I don't
know, it's not the same. He's not a beggar."

Bram laughed. "And how is that different, little lass?"

"It's not funny," Cammi said. "In your world, why are people beggars?"

Jandia shrugged. "Why am I a warrior? Why is Mirak a
bard? It is their job. They are beggars. That is how it is."

"Here, that's not how it is," insisted Cammi. Then, realizing that all were watching him, he closed up. "I'm sorry. I
was just—"

"That's all right, Cammi," said Gerontius gently. "Please
proceed."

Cammi looked at his friends. "We've been taught that any
one of us could be in his place. Maybe he lost his real job.
Maybe there was a fire and he lost all his possessions."

"Or he has mental issues," added Persephone. "People who
are mentally ill and can't get help sometimes end up on the
street. It's sad."

"Your society can create magic mirrors and wagons that
move on their own and glass towers that seem to graze the
heavens themselves, but cannot find houses for those in
need?" asked Torgrim. "This seems strange."

"Don't ask us to explain it," said Ralph. "We're just kids."

Noel pointed to the olive drab duffel bag at the man's feet.
"He might even be a veteran."

"What is a veteran?" asked Mirak.

"Someone who fought for our country and came home," explained Jojo.

Jandia looked amazed. "You mean to tell me when warriors return from battle in your world, they are not given feasts and great rewards?"

"Not always," said Ralph.

Jandia set her mouth in a hard line. "This is unjust."

"Yes, it is," said Persephone, who looked like she was going to cry. "I think we should help him."

The group crossed to where the man was standing.

He looked up and Ralph took him in. He was wrapped in loose clothing, with rags around his feet. Under a shapeless cloth cap, he had long dirty hair, maybe gray, maybe white. His face was lined, perhaps with age, but perhaps he had just led a hard life on the streets. He did not seem at all surprised to see the adventurers in their odd clothing with the five children.

"Spare change?" he asked in a low, quiet rasp.

Persephone reached into her pocket and pulled out a few quarters.

"Thank you, and have a blessed day," he said, and looked away. It seemed as though that was all he was after.

"Pardon, good sir, but we were wondering if you had anything to tell us?" asked Mirak in her soft, melodious voice.

He looked her full in the face. "Spare change?"

She gestured to Persephone, who scrounged around in her pockets and came up with a few more quarters. She placed them in his palm.

They waited expectantly.

"Thank you, and have a blessed day," the man repeated, just as before.

Ralph looked at Gerontius and gestured toward the street. "I think that's all he's going to say."

The group turned to go.

"Perhaps a few coppers or a piece of steel?" the man called out after them.

Bram's head snapped back. "Coppers you say?"

The man looked straight into the halfling's eyes.

"Coppers, or steel, it makes no difference." There was a hint of a smile around his eyes.

Bram carefully pulled the sack from around his neck and handed it to the man.

He weighed it in his hand and nodded. "This will do."

The kids exchanged glances.

Noel shook his head. "RPG, you should have known. I mean, in *every* adventure . . ."

"I know, Noel," snapped Ralph. "But who would have thought—"

"But, like, it totally makes sense for us to be standing here with an elf wizard, a dwarf cleric, and a halfling?" Jojo interjected.

"Quiet!" hissed Torgrim.

The thin man turned to Gerontius. "You seek the serpent."

"Yes, that is correct," the wizard answered.

"There is great danger there," the man said.

"We do not fear danger," said Jandia. "We seek it."

"Whoa! How cool is that?" said Noel.

"I know, right?" said Jojo, grinning.

"Hush, young ones!" admonished Mirak.

"The place you seek. It is . . ." He seemed distracted by Jandia's cape. "That fur on your cape? It is rabbit?"

"I would wear no rabbit on my person!" Jandia said

indignantly. "This is the fur of a wolf I killed with my bare hands as a child. I wear it to honor her."

"Accept my apologies," murmured the thin man. "I thought it was Belgian rabbit."

"Enough with this foolishness." Torgrim bristled. "What of the place?"

"Thank you, and have a blessed day," said the thin man, and his eyes turned inward again. He looked away from them.

"This is nonsense!" sputtered Torgrim. "You have told us nothing!"

Bram pulled him away. "My friend. He has told us much. You needed only to listen."

Gerontius agreed. "We must discuss this. To your house, Arpy. We will feast and talk of our next moves."

33

A PLAN OR A PLOT?

When they got to the apartment, Ralph made sure GG hadn't come home early. Not that that ever was going to happen, but he couldn't be too careful. There was no way to explain five strange-looking people tearing apart a deli plate in their living room.

Thankfully, the coast was clear, and just as Ralph had expected, the table manners of their guests were horrific. Chunks of deli meats and cheeses were flying everywhere, with slices of bread going down throats barely having been chewed.

Cammi looked like he was going to be sick. "I never really thought about how gross it was going to be," he managed to get out, heading to the kitchen and staying as far away as possible from the pillaging horde.

Torgrim, wiping his sleeve across the remains of what appeared to be half a jar of mustard on his beard, pronounced, "The food is admirable."

"Yes, but whatever was in these bottles bore very little resemblance to what we call ale in our world." Mirak eyed the table skeptically.

Jandia said it tasted like a horse had peed in it, but used a much ruder word, to no one's surprise. It didn't stop her from downing three bottles and belching loudly.

Ralph started to pick up the plates and put them in a plastic bag to leave in the trash can outside so his parents wouldn't ask any questions when they got home.

Gerontius looked up with a curious expression. "Why are you doing the work of the servants? This is beneath you."

"First off," Ralph replied, "we don't have any servants. Well, my sister and I feel like servants sometimes, but really we're just a family."

"No servants? But surely you are joking," said Bram. "A house of this size? At least a serving wench or two."

"No serving wenches, present company included," Jojo said firmly as she gingerly threw a half-eaten cocktail frank into the bag.

"So you are poor?" asked Jandia, getting right to the point as usual.

Noel laughed. "I wouldn't say RPG is poor. It's just that people like us don't have servants. Maybe a babysitter to help out if both parents work."

"This place grows stranger and stranger!" exclaimed Mirak. "You hire people to sit on your babies? In our world, we have a nursemaid, who tends to them with love and kindness."

"I would think that sitting on babies would be dangerous," reasoned Jandia, "but perhaps the babies are wearing armor of some kind to protect them."

"A babysitter sits *with* the baby, not *on* them," Persephone said as patiently as she could. "But I guess it is an odd word, now that I think of it."

Ralph could feel the conversation spiraling out of control. "Look, we need to get you out of here."

"This is a fine way to treat your guests, young lad," said Bram as he slid three packages of crackers into his vest.

"The thing is, my parents aren't going to understand who you are and why you're here," Ralph said. "They'll call the magistrates and it's going to be hard to explain."

Noel looked at Ralph. "The Beveren."

Jojo and Persephone looked confused.

Ralph rolled his eyes. In all the excitement and confusion, he'd completely forgotten.

"Of course," he said, "and we even have the money."

"Why does that word sound so familiar?" asked Cammi.

"Because it's the name of the hotel in downtown Brooklyn where the Reign of Dragons convention is being held tomorrow," Ralph said. "The one I've been trying to get all of you to go to for months."

"Dragon what?" asked Torgrim as the other adventurers leaned in.

"There are dragons about?" asked Jandia excitedly.

"Not exactly. It's hard to explain. But it's a gathering of people who all play—well, who all like the same things we do," said Ralph. He then remembered the cosplayers. "And even better! There are people who dress like you, so you'll fit right in!"

"This gathering is tomorrow?" asked Gerontius.

"Yes, and it's held in a place with many rooms for sleeping, and some for large groups—kind of like a gigantic inn," said Noel carefully.

"Is this enough to get us a room for the night?" asked Torgrim, holding up the ten hundred-dollar bills.

"I think so," said Ralph.

"Yep," said Jojo, looking at her phone. "According to their website, the suites are five hundred."

Bram stared at her phone covetously. "You were able to get that information from that little magic screen?"

Jojo reddened. "Um, yeah. It's really not that hard."

"I heard her say something about a web," Jandia said to Gerontius. "You are able to read omens in spiderwebs as well, are you not, Wizard?"

"That is true," Gerontius said, "but that is a very powerful magic. And my magic does not seem to work here."

"Uh-oh. There's kind of a problem," Jojo said, scrolling down the screen on her phone. "It says in big letters that costumes are only allowed in the convention area. They're forbidden in the lobby."

"Okay, so how are we getting them to the Beveren?" asked Persephone. "It's a good fifteen-minute walk from here, right? And they won't be allowed to check in looking like this."

"And we haven't even figured out what that beggar's prophecy means," protested Mirak. "Until we do that, I do not feel safe."

"I agree. Clearly it was a warning," added Torgrim.

Ralph now had two problems on his hands. "Let's tackle this one at a time. First off, how do we disguise them? Hold on." He turned to Cammi. "Are there costumes at the school?"

Cammi pulled the bill of his baseball cap down while he

thought for a moment. "I'm so sorry. I can't think of anything we have in the shop that would even fit them. Maybe a cowboy or gangster outfit from the last few shows, but that would only fit Bram."

"Wait a minute," Persephone said. She pointed to Jojo's sweatpants. "What about something like this?"

Noel snorted. "That's a great idea. Like, where are we going to find sweatshirts and sweatpants big enough for these guys? I doubt Ralph has them lying around."

"No! But I know where we can get them!" Ralph said. "Morrell's!"

"The sporting goods store?" asked Jojo. Then she brightened. "That's genius! It's just up a little bit past Court Street. And they have all kinds of sizes! Let's go!"

Ralph turned to their guests. "We are going out to get you suitable clothing. This way you can walk to the great inn undetected."

"We need to get you sweatshirts, hoodies, and sweatpants," Cammi added.

"And maybe some underwear," said Jojo nervously, looking at Jandia and Torgrim.

Gerontius stepped over to the kids. He leaned down, looking troubled. "What is it you are plotting? You are using words and phrases that are foreign to us."

"Gerontius is suspicious," said Bram. "As well he should be. So far you have treated us as friends and companions, knowing so much about us. But perhaps this is all a ruse to get us to let down our guard."

Torgrim spoke up. "They talk of leaving us here. They will go to the authorities themselves and betray us."

Jandia rose to her feet. "This is all true. We have put our trust in children. I do not even trust you, Bram."

"Sit down, Barbarian," Mirak said gently, turning to Persephone and smiling. It was still a bit unnerving to see her smile with those huge tusklike teeth, but they were getting used to it. "Persephone," she went on, reaching out and taking the girl by the arm, "tell me the truth."

"You are asking that one the truth?" muttered Bram. "I am witness to her ability to lie as well as any rogue I have ever known."

"I wasn't lying!" protested Persephone, looking mad. "I was acting. There's a difference."

"Oh, enlighten me, young one!" said Bram. "What, pray tell, makes what you did different from lying?"

"I don't know. It was pretending. I wasn't lying! I swear!" said Persephone.

Mirak gazed into her eyes. "This one will not lie to me," she said finally. "I would stake my life on it."

"And our lives as well," muttered Torgrim, who regarded Persephone suspiciously.

"We will not betray you," Persephone promised. "We would never do that. You are . . . our friends."

Bram snorted. "If I had a copper for every friend I've betrayed!"

"You have never betrayed us, Rogue," Torgrim said meaningfully.

"Because I would not rest until I had hunted him down and ripped his ears off his silly head," Jandia said happily. "Is that not right, Halfling?"

"Well, that's part of it. I do have a sense of loyalty to those who have protected me, and with whom I have shared so much. But these younglings . . ."

"We just need to get you disguises so you can sneak into the hotel without the authorities stopping you. What about this?" asked Ralph. "Only Jojo and I go. The others stay back with you."

"As hostages!" Jandia cried happily. "Yes! This is making sense."

"Not as hostages," Persephone said. "As friends."

"That is fine and it is settled," said Gerontius. "If you return with the articles of clothing, then all will be well."

Mirak bowed to them. "And if you bring anyone else with you—"

"We will kill our hostages!" added Jandia.

Noel and Cammi gasped.

"She did not mean that," Torgrim said quickly.

"I am sorry," Jandia said, putting her arm around Persephone. "I meant we will kill our friends."

34

THE GAME IS DISCOVERED

With the help of Cammi's expert eye, they were able to figure out the approximate sizes of the five visitors. At least with sweats they wouldn't need to be too exact.

Heading to Morrell's, Ralph and Jojo decided that it was probably better not to tell Bram and Torgrim that they had shopped for them in the children's section.

"And what happens after we convince them to put these clothes on?" Jojo asked.

"We get them to the Beveren hotel as quickly as possible, and hope at that point we can find someone who can help us find a Belgian rabbit, whatever that means," Ralph said.

"Maybe the last serpent swallowed a rabbit?" Jojo said.

Ralph held the door to the sporting goods store open and shook his head. "Jeez, and I thought Noel had all the dumb ideas."

It wasn't hard at all to find the clothing they needed, but as they waited to pay at the cashier, Ralph stopped short. "This isn't going to work."

Jojo glared at him. "Why not?"

"First off, how are we going to carry their weapons? The hotel has security guards. And who are we going to say they are when we check them in?"

"Now you figure that out?" Jojo said, throwing the pile of clothes she was carrying on the floor.

"Wait," Ralph said, closing his eyes. "I can do this. It's only a readjustment. Like when Cammi had those two dragons fall in love."

"Yeah, you handled that pretty well. But this isn't the game, RPG."

"We just have to look at what resources we have. And the strengths of our characters," explained Ralph. "Give me a minute." He smiled. "Okay, I think I've got it. We need to make a few more stops."

"Cool. So what is it?" asked Jojo.

"I'll tell you when we get home," Ralph said.

"Why can't you tell me now?"

"It's kind of complicated, and I need to make sure of a few things," Ralph said as they paid for the merchandise and watched as it was bagged up.

"You know, a couple of years ago I would have pushed you down and sat on you," Jojo said. "I kind of miss those days."

"I don't," Ralph said. He motioned across the street. "That's our next stop."

Morrell's was in the section of downtown Brooklyn called Fulton Mall, where everyone from all over the borough came to shop. There were new fancy high-fashion stores coming in and elbowing out the older bargain stores, but thankfully quite a few still remained, like the one Ralph and Jojo headed into, which sold school uniforms of all kinds for parents whose sons and daughters attended Brooklyn Catholic schools.

After making their purchases, Ralph looked relieved. "That wasn't too expensive. Now all we need is a street vendor." They were all over the place, selling knockoffs of designer bags, sunglasses, and scarves.

"Right over there." Jojo pointed. "I wish I knew what this was all about."

"You will," said Ralph.

"You know, I could still punch you in the stomach if I wanted," Jojo suggested. "For old times' sake."

"Okay! I'll tell you on the way home!" Ralph said.

Arms filled with shopping bags, Ralph and Jojo rushed back to Garden Place and up the steps to the parlor floor.

Jojo hit the doorbell with her elbow. She was smiling. "You know, I have to hand it to you. That's pretty ingenious."

"If it works," Ralph said as Cammi opened the door. He looked worried, but that wasn't unusual, as he looked worried most of the time.

"It wasn't my fault," Cammi said immediately.

Inside, the adventurers looked dazed, staring into space.

"It was Noel!" Persephone said with annoyance.

"What was Noel?" asked Ralph. And then he saw the table and dropped the bags.

"Hey, I just told them the truth," Noel said, shrugging. "I had to say something."

Gerontius was holding the character sheets in his hands.

The ones that described each of their characters, down to the color of their hair and their health points.

"Okay, what happened?" Ralph asked.

"Bram was poking around and saw the table with the minis on it and realized they were miniature versions of them," Noel started. "He showed the character sheets to Gerontius, who asked me what they were, and I told them the truth."

"You keep saying that," Ralph said. "What exactly is the truth?"

"That they were characters in a game that we made up," Noel said as if it was no big thing.

Gerontius turned slowly and faced Ralph. "This is not so. We are real. We exist. What Noel has told us is some kind of joke, is it not?"

Ralph took a deep breath. "It's a little hard to explain. You see—"

"My sword is real," growled Jandia. "I can prove it."

Mirak raised her hand. "Stay your blade, Jandia. This is some sort of dark magic. We do not know what we are dealing with, and these children did say they were our friends. Did you not mean it?"

"We did! We are! It's not exactly magic. Well, or maybe it is. At least, it's not our magic."

Torgrim approached Ralph with a stricken look on his face. "Please, youngling, do not speak in riddles. Tell us what is happening." He gestured to the tabletop, where the figures were arrayed on a map. "We see the temple, the Kreel. How is it possible that you know our adventures so well?"

Ralph felt a prickling sensation on his skin. The others of his group had gathered behind him.

Gerontius's eyes bored into him. "Please explain the meaning of Noel's words."

"I . . . I . . . I . . . can't," Ralph said. "All I can tell you is that we play a game where we make up heroes and give them attributes. We have been playing as you five for two years now. So I guess you could say, from our perspective at least, that we made you up."

"Two years!" cried Bram. "The boy lies. We all have memories. We have been on our world for tens of years. A century, in the case of Torgrim. They cannot have made that up. My childhood, my family, my past! I have a sister named—"

"Gloriana," Gerontius said.

Bram turned white. "I have never uttered her name, in all our adventures."

Gerontius held up a sheet. It had the words *Bram, Halfling Rogue* scrawled on it. "It is written here. Along with the names of your parents, Dionne and Davoth."

"Who wrote this?" Bram demanded.

Noel grinned. "I did. I like to be thorough, so I put in a lot of details that aren't always used in the game."

Mirak picked up the papers Ralph had been using to plot their campaign. She read off the coversheet. "'The Search for the Seven Serpents of the House of Cormorant.'" She looked up. "This is our story. You have been telling our story?"

"How does it end?" asked Jandia.

"We haven't gotten there yet."

"They do not control our lives!" thundered Torgrim, shaking with rage. "Orach'T'char guides me."

"I cannot believe that we were created by you. That our lives have been controlled by a group of children. This is madness. We have had full lives and made all our own choices, not you." Gerontius's voice was calm, but there was something behind it. The wizard was trying to make sense of what they had been told.

"Well, we don't control everything," Persephone said.

"Ah!" said Mirak, "Gerontius, this is something. We are not mere puppets. Even if these children have somehow put us in our world, we have our free will. We make the choices that rule our destinies."

"Well, actually, the dice guide you," Noel explained patiently, as if he were teaching Reign of Dragons to a dumb grown-up.

"The dice?" said Bram, picking one up.

"Noel, you're not helping," Jojo said. "Let RPG explain."

"It's just that . . . well, when we get to certain places in the game and you have an opportunity to perform a given action, we roll the dice to see if you've succeeded or failed."

"Like breaking into a dungeon, trying to convince people of stuff, or, obviously, combat," added Noel, which only made it worse.

Jandia drew herself up to loom over Noel. "This is not so, child. I am the one who fights. I am the one who bleeds, or causes others to bleed. My skill is not based on chance or the whims of a child."

Jojo rushed over to her. "Yes, you do fight. And because of your high strength number, you usually succeed. You are a great warrior, Jandia Ravenhelm."

Jandia softened. Then her face showed confusion. "High number?"

"When we roll the dice, you add your strength number,"

Ralph said, "and that usually is enough to, um, vanquish the foe."

Gerontius held his head in his hands. He took a deep breath. He then laughed. A single dark croak with no humor in it. "Our lives are in the hands of children rolling dice. This is more than I can bear."

The adventurers gathered in a circle, looking at one another. Torgrim grabbed his amulet and shut his eyes tight. "I call upon you, Orach'T'char, to protect us, guide us. Give me the perception and wisdom to see the truth."

After a moment, he opened his eyes. "There is no answer. My god does not answer." His shoulders sagged, and he began to sniffle.

"This is not good," said Persephone.

"I don't know how to fix it," Ralph said. "But they need to be out of here in an hour or my parents are going to have a lot of questions."

"Hey, guys, I just had a crazy thought," Noel said. "You want to hear it?"

"Not really," said Cammi.

Noel went on, unfazed. "What if we're characters in someone else's game? You know, and we just don't know it?"

"Don't be stupid," said Jojo. "We're real."

"They thought they were real," Noel said, pointing to the adventurers.

"You mean, someone somewhere could be rolling dice to determine our futures?" asked Cammi.

"Sure. Wouldn't that be crazy?" said Noel.

"Yeah . . . crazy," said Ralph, trying not to think about all that that meant.

There was silence as the kids pondered this. It was ridiculous. And yet . . . that was what the adventurers had thought. And here they were.

Ralph sat down on the floor and realized that the others had suddenly sat down too. No one knew what to say.

It seemed to last forever. The moment of realization. The feelings were so intense, so ridiculous, and yet so possible at the same time. It was like nothing they had ever felt before.

What was real? Was there a character sheet somewhere that said *Ralph Peter Ginzberg* in some kid's handwriting? Was there a board of Brooklyn Heights with miniature versions of Noel, Persephone, Jojo, Cammi, and him on it? Who was the game master? It was all too much.

Suddenly, out of the dead quiet, there was a sound.

It was a beautiful single note plucked from a harp.

It was joined by a second, and then a chord.

There was another sound now, low and soothing.

They let Mirak's voice wash over them. The sound was both ancient and new, as if no one had ever sung that song before and yet they had known it their entire life.

Ralph became aware that it had been joined by a younger, higher voice.

He looked up to see that Persephone had moved over to Mirak and rested her head on the bard's shoulder.

They sang in perfect harmony, the two voices rising and falling together, creating something that healed and seemed to tell them that all was possible, that there was magic even in Brooklyn Heights.

When the song was over, the last sweet notes hung in the air, filling the empty room.

Persephone hugged Mirak, who grabbed the young girl in a firm embrace. "We have made music together," she said simply. "And that is powerful."

Ralph got to his feet and took Gerontius's hand. It was soft, yet had great strength in it. Ralph squeezed it.

Gerontius met his gaze. He squeezed back.

"You are real," Ralph said. "We are real. There is still a quest to be fulfilled. And we must do it."

Gerontius nodded. "Wise words, Arpy. We are called here for a reason."

"You know, I still don't think we're the ones who summoned them," said Noel slowly.

"I think you're right," said Ralph. "Someone or something has put you here and used us to get you to the right place."

There was a horrible noise, a disgusting wet sound.

Jojo had brought some tissues over to Torgrim, who was blowing his nose.

"He was about to use the drapes," Jojo said, shrugging.

"We need a plan," Bram said.

"Ralph has a plan," Jojo said, "and it's a good one!"

"If only we knew what the Belgian rabbit was that the beggar referred to," Ralph said as he gathered their things. "I know that's the key to getting us where we need to go."

Cammi was busy on his phone. He looked up with a big smile, the kind that said he knew something the others didn't.

Persephone's eyes narrowed. "Okay, Cammi. What have you got?"

"I just looked up Belgian rabbit on my phone to see the names of the breed."

"And?" asked Jojo.

Cammi held out his phone. "You'll never guess what the most common one is!"

Noel rushed over and shook his head. "Yeah, of course."

The best-known Belgian rabbit was the Beveren.

35

WHY ARE THESE WOMEN STARVING?

"**R**PG, what the heck are you doing?"

Ralph turned from the computer screen in his room to yell downstairs back to Jojo. "I'm just finishing up."

He carefully printed out the receipt for the hotel reservation he'd made in the name of Reign Productions and headed downstairs. He couldn't wait to see what Cammi had come up with.

It wasn't easy to explain to the adventurers what a photo shoot was or how they would pretend to be part of one.

Persephone had shown them pictures in one of GG's many fashion magazines.

Jandia looked and said, "This is very sad. Are all these pictures of pale, starving women to get people to send them food?"

"Um, they're actually admired for their beauty," Jojo said, sounding a little embarrassed.

"They don't look happy," Mirak said, turning the pages

and seeing face after pouting face staring back at her with huge, icy eyes. "I have seen expressions like that, but only on women who have been bewitched."

"Perhaps they are undead," suggested Bram from across the room.

"Hold still!" said Cammi through a mouthful of pins. They had found Ralph's mother's sewing kit, and he was busy adjusting the blazer Ralph had gotten at the uniform store. Before Cammi had gotten started, it had hung on Bram like a sack, but with a little pulling in at the waist, he almost looked like the self-important personal assistant he was going to play.

"So I am a portrait painter?" Gerontius had asked.

"Kind of," Noel said, clicking the shutter of an old digital camera that belonged to Ralph's parents. "But this, um, magic box is able to paint the portrait in a matter of seconds."

Gerontius gazed at the screen on the back with astonishment. "Such amazing sorcery," he murmured.

Torgrim and Noel were bringing cases up from the cellar just as Ralph reached the bottom of the stairs.

When they started their business, Ralph's parents had lugged their own equipment from one commercial shoot to another. Backdrops, cameras, tripods, everything. Nowadays, they just rented it.

Thankfully they hadn't gotten around to selling their old equipment; they'd just stowed it downstairs. And the cases were exactly what the kids needed: the large, tubelike case that held the backdrops and frame fit the swords and bow perfectly. They even had a dolly to wheel it all on. Torgrim's chain mail and helmet fit into one duffel bag, and the robes of the others fit into another. There was a large hard-shell case that was just right for Torgrim's war hammer, and they were done.

"I need to be able to move," Jandia complained. "This is too tight." Cammi had put her in a small sweatshirt and leggings, which emphasized her strong thighs and calves.

"You look great!" said Persephone, who was putting up Jandia's hair.

Jandia scowled. "Why does he get to keep his cape?"

Cammi sighed as he adjusted Gerontius's pants. Since the elf was so slim, they had decided to get him women's sizes, which he somehow still made look elegant. His ears would be a problem, so they'd gotten him a beanie to hide them. He definitely looked eccentric.

"He's supposed to be the photographer, so he's allowed to look a little . . . different," Ralph explained.

Jojo reached into the bag and got out the accessories they'd bought at the street vendor.

She handed Cammi a bandana, which he carefully wrapped around the large head of the dwarf.

"What is my role, Arpy?" Torgrim asked.

"You are what's called the assistant to the photographer," said Ralph. "You help with carting all the bags and basically setting up the shoot."

"I am a servant?" growled Torgrim. "A servant to the wizard? Absolutely not."

"It's a part," Persephone said with irritation. "We keep telling you, you're just pretending."

"I love it!" said Bram, preening around the room.

"You would." Mirak smiled. "It's what you do best."

"Why isn't the bard a servant?" groused Torgrim.

"She is the producer," Ralph tried. He had given up explaining all the roles to everyone's satisfaction. The only one who was important was Bram.

Noel remembered that one of his most powerful skills was the ability to impersonate anyone. So he would do all the talking.

They had showed him a video entitled "Behind the Scenes of a Commercial Shoot" on Jojo's phone. Once he and the others had gotten over the marvel of moving pictures on a screen, Bram watched it a few times and then nodded. It was uncanny how he had internalized the speaking patterns and the mannerisms of an arrogant celebrity supermodel's assistant.

He cleared his throat. "Listen, man, have you any idea what the budget is on this shoot? We're running behind as it is!" Bram looked at the children.

Persephone clapped her hands. "That was amazing. Perfection."

Bram glowed. "I suppose if I knew what any of it meant it would be better, but this will have to do."

Cammi moved over to Mirak and arranged the long scarf they had gotten at the street vendor around her neck, puffing it up so it would hide her lower jaw. In his expert hands, it had become both a disguise and a fashion statement.

Cammi stepped back. "Well, I wish I had more time. I'm sorry. . . ."

"What are you saying?" Persephone said. "They look great!"

It was true. Cammi had somehow transformed the group of ancient adventurers into a hip team of fashionable creative types who would be checking into the hotel for a photo shoot.

"What if we need to do battle on the way?" Jandia asked.

She was reaching into the large case and grabbing her sword. After a few tries, she was satisfied she could reach it in seconds. "I still do not feel right about leaving here swordless."

"I will protect you, my lady," Bram said. He opened the blazer to reveal that he was still wearing Salt and Pepper strapped to his shirt.

"Somehow I do not feel better."

"You used a funny word to describe Jandia," Mirak said to Jojo. "What was it you called her?"

"A supermodel," Jojo responded.

"No, it was another word," Gerontius said.

"We called her the star," Persephone said, "because she is."

Jandia looked uncomfortable. "I am no star. I do not shine."

"But you do, my barbarian queen," said Bram. "Brighter than any in the sky."

"Enough with your jokes, or I will cut out your tongue," snapped Jandia. But there was a small smile on her face. "Lying rogue."

Ralph took one last look around the living room. It was now three-thirty. An hour and a half to get them into the hotel and figure out their next step.

His friends had helped him clean everything up and make it look almost as if no one had been there. All the trash was in a large plastic bag they would deposit in a public trash can on their way to the hotel.

As a last touch, Ralph handed out hip-looking dark glasses, knockoffs from the street.

Gerontius looked at them, confused.

"They're sunglasses," said Noel. "Put them on."

"But we're inside," Torgrim protested.

"You wear them everywhere," Cammi explained.

"But that makes no sense," said Mirak. "If they are sunglasses, shouldn't they—"

"Yes!" said Jojo through gritted teeth. "It doesn't make sense. It's fashion. It's not supposed to make sense."

The adventurers put on their sunglasses.

Ralph and the others stepped back and marveled at the transformation.

Jojo snapped a photo of them. She turned and showed the visitors. "Looking pretty sharp, right?"

Jandia gasped. "It is an image of us! Frozen in time."

Gerontius was about to speak, when Ralph held up his hand. "We know. 'What sorcery is this?'"

"Actually, I was going to say it was a lovely likeness," Gerontius sniffed.

"Yeah, right. You were totally going to say that," drawled Bram, in his "assistant's voice." He turned to the kids and winked.

"You're so good at that it's scary," said Persephone.

"You're not so bad yourself, sweetheart," he answered, adjusting his blazer and pushing his glasses up onto his head. He definitely had the look down.

Ralph glanced at his watch. They had an hour. Plenty of time to get to the hotel, check them in, and get home before his parents.

This was going to work. No one would ever know about it.

Except GG, who had just come through the front door.

36

OH, *THAT* JANDIA

"**W**e are betrayed!" exclaimed Jandia, reaching for the tube that held her sword.

"It's my sister!" Ralph said, grabbing her arm.

"Ralph, you want to tell me what's going on?" GG said, eyeing the strange-looking people surrounding her.

All eyes turned to Ralph. "They're friends of Mom and Dad's. You met them at that holiday party last year."

GG looked dubious. "I don't remember—"

"GG!" Ralph said. He pulled her aside. "Sure you do. That group that stayed by themselves in the corner? The ones everyone was talking about?" He desperately hoped some of Bram's skill at bluffing had rubbed off on him.

"I . . . think so. The tall dude with the gray hair looks familiar. Did he do a job with them?"

"Yes!" Ralph said, as if this were the most obvious thing in the world. "Of course he did."

"What was his name, again?" GG whispered.

"Gerontius!" Ralph said. "How could you ever forget a name like that?"

"Right . . . ," GG said. She turned and addressed the group. "Gerontius! Right?"

Behind her back, Ralph gave a "just play along" look to Gerontius.

"Great to see you again!" GG continued. "I'm so sorry my folks aren't here."

"Yes, well . . . we took a chance," Gerontius said.

Bram stepped forward. "Hey, babe. Bummed your parents aren't here. We were so stoked about shooting your parents."

GG looked confused.

"Oh, you're so funny!" said Persephone, laughing incredibly convincingly. "He meant to say 'meet' and said 'shoot' instead!"

"They're so jet-lagged," said Jojo quickly. "We were just walking them a little way to their hotel."

"Wow, that's pretty impressive," GG said to Gerontius. "Usually nothing will pry them away from their game."

"Yes, the game," Gerontius said, smiling weakly.

GG shook her head. "You should see these guys pretending to be wizards and barbarians and stuff. They're so into it."

"It sounds like a lot of fun," said Mirak pleasantly.

"Have you ever played?" asked Torgrim, adjusting his bandana.

GG laughed. "Me? Yeah, I don't think so. I can't see myself hanging out with a bunch of wizards and bards or whatevers. That's not going to happen."

"Oh, you'd be surprised," said Noel. "You never know."

Ralph had a feeling Noel would be too tempted to give more away if they stayed much longer.

"We'll be right back," Ralph said. "I have my phone. We're just walking them partway to the Beveren."

"I dunno . . . I should check with Mom and Dad first," GG said, taking out her phone.

"GG, don't bother them on a shoot with something like this," Ralph said. "The last time, Mom got all mad because they were in the middle of a crisis, remember?"

GG thought for a minute. "I guess that's true. But if you're not home by the time they get here, I'm not covering for you."

"It's literally going to be like fifteen minutes!" Ralph said.

"Just make sure you're back, because I'm not dealing with anyone else's parents," GG said.

The other parents. Great. One more thing for them to worry about.

Jojo pulled at Jandia's sleeve. "Okay, guys. We're off."

Torgrim grunted as he pushed the dolly down the stairs to the street, followed by the others.

The bored young man in the black form-fitting T-shirt was aimlessly flipping through the pages of a fashion magazine when he looked up to discover an amazing scene at his welcome desk at the Beveren. He had gotten used to all the geeks and nerds who had been checking into the cheapest rooms in anticipation of tomorrow's convention, for whatever corny board-game thing the hotel had booked. He was glad he was off in fifteen minutes.

But these were no nerds or geeks. Instead he was greeted with the sight of a group of fashionistas, as the staff called them. From the looks of the luggage, they were here for a shoot.

He smiled as a small man in a blazer approached.

"Well, hey there, Gorgo," said Bram, peering at the name tag on the young man's shirt. "We'd like to check in as soon as possible."

"I'd be delighted to help you," the young man said, adding acidly, "It's pronounced 'Giorgio,' by the way."

Bram gave him another huge smile. "You know, I really don't care how it's pronounced, Gorgo. I have a photo shoot to arrange with an international supermodel, and every minute is costing me money."

Giorgio snapped to attention. "Of course, sir. May I have your reservation number and credit card?"

Ralph handed the sheet to Bram and whispered in his ear. Bram nodded. "Here's the reservation information."

Giorgio typed the information in and nodded. "Very good, sir! Now all I need is that credit card."

"We will be paying in cash," said Bram, pulling out a roll of bills from his pocket.

Giorgio turned slightly pale. "This is rather irregular. We usually require a credit card."

Luckily, Ralph had already rehearsed Bram on this possibility.

Bram leaned in, and said in a low voice, "Listen, this is for a Japanese magazine. *Kawaii Kitty Girl*. Perhaps you've heard of it?"

Giorgio looked confused for a moment.

"Ah." Bram sighed. "It's really only read by the hippest people in the business. So it's not surprising that—"

"Of course I've heard of it!" protested Giorgio. "I have a subscription!" Seeing as there was no such magazine, it was clear that Bram wasn't the only one who was good at bluffing.

Giorgio looked over at Jandia, who was tossing her hair about and doing her best to remember all the things Cammi had taught her. She pouted and tried to look as unhappy as all the starving women in the magazines they'd shown her.

"She looks so familiar," Giorgio said, trying to catch her eye.

"That's Jandia," explained Bram.

Giorgio looked confused. He thought he knew the names of all the supermodels in the business. "Is she new?"

"I'm sorry. Maybe you didn't hear me. She's Jandia?" Bram said, looking over his dark glasses in shock.

Giorgio immediately nodded. "Ohhh . . . of course. Jandia. Please forgive me. She looks different in person." He yelled out to her, "Welcome to the Beveren! I'm Giorgio!"

Jandia bared her teeth at him.

"Wow. She is fierce, isn't she?" said Giorgio.

"You don't know the half of it," said Bram pleasantly.

"We still need your credit card and you'll be on your way," Giorgio said.

"As you know," Bram said conspiratorially, "these companies pay for everything in cash. Tax purposes. Makes things easier for everyone. You understand, of course?" Bram asked.

He peeled a fifty-dollar bill from his roll and put it between himself and Giorgio. "I would really appreciate your help in this matter, Gorgo."

Giorgio looked around and put his hand over the money. Hey, for fifty bucks, the little guy could call him Gorgo.

"All right," he said, typing a few more things on his keyboard. "I think we're all set. I'll need a cash deposit as security in case of damages."

Bram took the roll of cash and spread it out on the counter. "Will this do?"

Giorgio coughed. "Yes, yes. Very nicely. Here you go! You have a suite of rooms on the eighteenth floor. Elevators to your left." He handed a set of key cards to Bram, who looked confused.

Ralph scooped up the cards and pulled at his sleeve. "Thanks so much."

"Wait, who are you?" Giorgio asked, eyeing the kids suspiciously.

"Um, we're . . . we're . . ." Ralph turned to Persephone for help.

Persephone knew what to do. Everyone always made assumptions about what Asian country she was from, and she bet this guy was no different. She swept to the front of the group and grabbed the key cards, then bowed.

Giorgio broke out into a big grin and bowed back. *"Irrashaimaste!"* he said proudly, mangling the Japanese welcome.

"Hai, Dozo," she answered.

"Her parents own the magazine," Ralph informed Giorgio, who nodded his understanding.

"So you're her friends," he reasoned.

"Exactly," said Jojo.

"I do hope you enjoy your stay," said Giorgio as they headed to the elevator banks.

"She looks so much skinnier in her photos," he mused as Jandia walked past.

"I didn't know you knew Japanese," Cammi said to Persephone.

"I only know that from when they greet you at a sushi bar," Persephone said. She glared at Ralph. "We were lucky that's all the Japanese he knew too."

"I panicked," said Ralph. "Sorry about making you do that."

"Just don't make a habit of it," Persephone said.

"But how are we to get all this up eighteen flights of stairs?" asked Torgrim, eyeing all their baggage.

Jojo sighed. "Don't worry. This is an elevator. We get into the box and press a button and it takes us up to our floor."

Jandia let out a low growl. She had been keeping herself in check for the entire walk over to the hotel, and even kept quiet as the men around her seemed to regard her as a piece of meat.

She was not going to be trapped in some box.

"I will check for traps," Bram promised as the door slid open. He gazed upward. "Look there!" He beamed. "An escape door. We can crawl up that if we have to."

Jandia relented, and they moved all their stuff into the car. Just as the doors were closing, a young couple entered.

The elevator smoothly moved upward, and the man whispered to Ralph, "That's Jandia, isn't it?"

Ralph tried not to look alarmed. "Why . . . yes. How did you know that?"

"The man at the desk told us," the woman said excitedly. "Do you think we could get a picture with her?"

"I don't think that's a great idea," Jojo chimed in. "She's a little touchy about that."

"I totally understand," the woman said as the doors opened. The band unloaded their gear and exited the elevator.

"We love your work!" the young man called after Jandia.

37

JUST AN ORDINARY DAY

It had taken longer than Ralph had hoped to settle the adventurers into their room.

Just explaining how to open the door was a challenge. He finally had to tell them the card was an enchanted scroll that needed to be inserted just the right way in order to gain access.

"Ah! So it is like the doors of the citadel of Maramount, with the mage's cards," said Gerontius.

The puzzle of the mage's cards. It was one of the first puzzles Declan had given them. Ralph remembered the thrill of victory when they had finally solved it.

"Yes." He smiled. "It's exactly like that."

He had made sure their provisions were taken care of, calling room service to set up their dinner. But simply teaching them how they were to pay for everything using cash was tricky. It was decided that Torgrim would handle the actual money (no one trusted Bram).

Noel had slightly better luck explaining the notion of the

bathroom and how it worked, which was causing a fair amount of confusion. They seemed to understand the bathtub, but the toilet was yet another cause for Gerontius to marvel at the magical properties of modern plumbing.

"You press this handle down," Cammi was explaining, "and it whooshes all your . . . stuff . . . away."

Jandia was totally unconvinced. "I will do it outside," she announced, "behind a tree, as always."

"No, you won't!" Persephone said firmly. "You are a super-model, remember that. Not a pet dog."

The kids said good night after making the adventurers promise to stay inside until morning. The fact that they would then be able to wear their own clothing helped convince them to wait to do their exploring.

"Once the other conventioneers show up, they should blend in perfectly," Cammi said happily in the elevator.

As they headed toward Ralph's house, Jojo pulled up short. "So . . . how is this going to work?"

"You mean tomorrow?" Ralph asked. He hadn't really thought about it. It was true that he was the only one who was planning to go to RoDCon.

"I mean, we don't even know what we're looking for," Jojo continued. "And I have plans."

"So break them," Noel said, looking at her impatiently. "I'm just telling my parents I changed my mind after playing all day. That's pretty simple."

Cammi looked worried. "I'm really sorry, guys, but Persephone has a rehearsal tomorrow. And I'm meeting with the costume teacher to pick out fabric for the costumes for the main characters."

Persephone's eyes lit up. "Food poisoning. We'll email and say that RPG fed us bad fish tacos or something."

Ralph made a face. "So it's my fault?"

"You have a better idea?" Persephone demanded. "Our parents don't have to know. They can drop us at school and you can meet us there."

Ralph admitted that it was a pretty solid plan.

They turned to Jojo, who looked irritated. "I said I can't."

"Come on, Jojo. What's going on that you're just going to abandon Jandia like that?"

Cammi piped up. "She's going to spend the day shopping with Joie and Twyla."

"You can't be serious," Ralph said. "You honestly are ticked off because—"

"You wouldn't understand," snapped Jojo. "I actually have a life, okay?"

Noel looked incredulous. "There are magical beings in a Brooklyn hotel and we are going to have an adventure trying to get them back to their own world. And you're mad because you can't go shopping."

"Fine. I'll be there," said Jojo.

They had arrived at the front door of Ralph's brownstone. Persephone's parents were talking to Jojo's mom. They were laughing about something.

"Oh, there you are!" Jojo's mother said, giving her a hug. "I was about to text you."

Persephone took in both her parents and Jojo's mom. "Sorry we took so long. We were watching a fashion shoot."

"That sounds cool," her father said, "but we really have to dash. Cammi, you're coming with us."

He nodded happily and jumped into their car. Cammi never had to explain where he was to his mom or grandmother. As a corporate lawyer, his mom was usually so busy with one case or another, he just spent his time with Persephone or Jojo or one of his other friends until his grandmother came home from the theater.

Noel looked up from his phone. His mother was on the way.

Ralph trudged up the stairs and saw GG coming down the block. She called to him, "Mom texted me to say they're running late and to heat up the leftover Chinese food."

Ralph nodded and looked at the scene in front of him, with his friends being picked up and driving off, just as if it had been any other session of RoD. It felt almost normal, as if the halfling rogue, elf wizard, dwarf cleric, half-orc bard, and barbarian human were safely tucked away in their imaginations, to be pulled out next week, instead of actually sitting in a hotel room fifteen blocks away, waiting until morning to discover the secret of their mission and why they had been summoned here.

38

BRAM SEEKS HIS REVENGE BUT IS THWARTED BY AN OVERBITE

Ralph turned to his friends as they stood in front of the hotel room door the next morning. "We'd better be ready for whatever happened in that room last night."

"Who knows if they're even in there?" said Noel, always happy to mention everyone's worst fear.

Jojo rolled her eyes. "I wish. Can we just get this over with?" She'd been a joy to be around ever since she'd met them in front of the school.

Ralph had been able to convince GG not to mention their parents' "friends," explaining that Gerontius and the others wanted to surprise them at dinner. If they were able to meet whoever they needed to meet or solve whatever they needed to solve here at the Beveren, he'd come up with something to explain their absence later. If this was just another clue leading them somewhere else, then it wouldn't matter anyway. The truth would have to come out.

He knocked tentatively on the door. There was the sound

of movement inside; the door opened, and he was relieved to see the group looking well rested and impressively adorned in their own clothes.

"And a very good morning to you, young ones!" Bram called out.

There were two trays pushed over by the window with what looked like the remains of a breakfast.

"You ate well?" Persephone asked.

"We ate like kings and queens!" exclaimed Mirak happily.

"The bath was quite extraordinary," Gerontius added. "There was abundant hot water for everyone. I could not find its source."

Torgrim was finishing up a piece of toast and patted his belly. "I have had better honey. But it was certainly satisfactory."

There was a flushing noise from the bathroom. Ralph and Jojo exchanged horrified glances.

Jandia appeared at the door. She had a huge smile on her face. "I am enjoying that very much!" she announced.

"She used it five times already," said Bram proudly.

"Good for you!" Jojo said, smiling back. "Are we ready to go?"

Jandia seemed unwilling to drop what clearly was her new favorite topic. "It is like sitting on a throne! But for—"

"Yes! We know what it's for!" Noel said quickly.

Jandia picked up her sword belt and strapped it on. She yawned and flexed her massive arms. "My bowels are empty and I am well fed. Let us go."

"Okay, then!" Ralph said, clapping his hands. "Anyone else? Everyone's bowels empty?"

The adventurers nodded.

"Then we're off!" he said, and led the way to the elevators that would take them down to the ballroom floor, where the convention took place.

On the way down, the elevator doors opened a few floors lower, and a couple of costumed conventioneers got on. They were dressed as elves, with homemade robes. They looked at their fellow passengers, impressed.

"I am Leontes, and this is Parsimon," one of them announced.

The adventurers smiled and shook their hands.

"Those are great teeth!" Leontes said to Mirak. "Whose are they?"

"They're mine," Mirak answered pleasantly.

Parsimon tried to clarify. "Right. But he meant where did you get them?"

"I was born with them," Mirak replied, looking at the strange human with the stuck-on ears.

Persephone pulled Leontes aside. "I'm sure you know people like her. She stays in character no matter what. She got them on the Internet."

"Ah. I see." Leontes nodded.

The doors opened, and they were greeted with a sight both strange and familiar.

Creatures from the Reign of Dragons universe were gathered in small groups throughout the large entryway. There were knights, wizards, orcs, elven archers, and even one or two halflings. All of them were in a line waiting to get their tickets to enter the great ballroom just beyond the high doors in the back of the room. Tables were set up with the organizers of the event giving out the tickets.

The group went to the end of the line, and Ralph tried to see if any of the other conventioneers were carrying anything resembling a golden serpent.

"Do you see anything?" Cammi asked Ralph, scanning the crowd.

"Nope." Ralph continued to look.

"It might not matter if we did," Noel said. "The Search for the Seven Serpent Scepter is one of the most beloved game modules in the Reign of Dragons world. Someone might have painted some wooden snake gold to bring as a prop."

"True," said Ralph.

The adventurers were seemingly taken aback.

"It is like a dream!" whispered Gerontius. "They are so like us, and yet not."

A number of fellow guests had already complimented them on their costumes, when Bram caught sight of someone.

"That purple cloak . . . with the silver sun emblazoned on it," he muttered. "It cannot be."

The owner of the cloak turned and revealed a green scaly head fitted with a steel helmet.

Bram gasped. "It is Orak-Thule! The killer of my people! I will have my revenge!"

"You don't think?" asked Jojo as the creature turned to face Bram and hissed.

Bram pulled Salt and Pepper out. "Orak-Thule! Prepare to meet thy death at the hands of Bram Quickfoot!"

"Rash words, Halfling!" the creature hissed, pulling out his sword.

People parted to give them room. "This is great!" an orc eating a bagel said to his friend dressed as a gnome.

"Wait, that's not really Orak-Thule, right?" Ralph said.

"I bet he's going to say 'This ends now!'" Noel said.

"This ends now!" cried Bram, and rushed the scaly creature, a knife in each hand.

"Told ya," said Noel.

The lizard-man slipped as he backed away, and suddenly his face jarred loose and sagged a little.

"Guys! He's wearing a mask!" Cammi called out.

Ralph ran to grab Bram's arm before he could do any damage. "Bram! Wait!"

Bram threw him off. "Leave off, boy. This is the moment I avenge the murder of my family."

The lizard-man swiveled his head and faced them. "Ralph? Is that you?" The creature pulled up his mask.

Ralph's eyes widened. "Bram! Hold your attack!" he cried. "That's not Orak-Thule! It's Dr. Falatko, my orthodontist!"

39

THIS WAY DOWN

Dr. Falatko thought it was all great fun, never having thought Bram's daggers were real. And he loved the adventurers. He was especially interested in Mirak. He peered at her lower teeth. "Those are real, aren't they?" he asked gently.

Mirak looked at the others and then nodded.

"I can help with that," Dr. Falatko offered, fishing around in his chain mail and then proffering his business card.

"Help with what?" asked Mirak, inspecting the card as if it were a relic of some kind.

"You know, fix your smile," he said. "With just the right dental procedures, you'd be quite a pretty young woman."

Jandia pushed her way to the front. "What's wrong with her now?" she demanded.

"Yeah!" added Jojo. "I think she looks great just the way she is."

The other kids glared at the doctor.

"Fine. I was just trying to help," Dr. Falatko said, shaking his head.

Mirak stared at him as he walked away. "In your world, it seems there is only one way to look beautiful. Is this so?"

"Not everybody feels that way." Cammi sighed. "But, yes, it's still pretty bad. We've got some work to do."

The line was moving briskly, and they had gotten to the front. There was a young man sitting at the table with a laptop in front of him, eating a doughnut. His name tag identified him as Gary Beard, Event Coordinator. He barely looked up when Torgrim placed his war hammer on the table.

"No props on the table, please," he said, unfazed.

Torgrim looked confused. "Prop? What do you mean?"

"You know, the hammer thing," Gary Beard said, pointing with what was left of the doughnut.

Torgrim gaped in astonishment. "Show respect, human. Deathbringer has been bathed in the blood of a thousand orcs, goblins, and Kreel. It has crushed the skulls of those who do not show the due deference it commands."

Gary Beard looked up, his expression unchanged. "Yeah, whatever. Remove it, please."

Noel tugged at Torgrim's sleeve. "Dude, do as he says. We just want to get by him, okay?"

"Consider this a lucky day," Torgrim growled at the man. "I will do as you ask."

Gary Beard indicated the line behind them. "Your names?"

Ralph moved to the front and showed his ticket. Gary Beard nodded and gave him a pass to hang around his neck.

"The others didn't buy theirs in advance," Ralph told him. "So we'll need nine more."

Gary Beard laughed. "Yeah, right. Good luck with that."

"What's so funny?" Jojo demanded.

"This has been sold out for weeks. Sorry." Gary Beard didn't sound sorry in the slightest.

Bram pushed forward. He smiled charmingly as he glanced at Gary Beard's name tag and then at the banner hung behind him that declared BROUGHT TO YOU BY MAGES OF THE MIDWEST. "There has clearly been some mistake . . . Gary, is it? We are special guests of the Mages of the Midwest."

"Oh yeah?" The man chuckled. "Who exactly invited you? Because I have all the special invitations right here." He pointed to a small box with envelopes in them.

Bram's fingers twitched. He made eye contact with Persephone, who started to wobble.

"Ohhh . . . I'm feeling dizzy . . . ," she said loudly.

"I told you you should have eaten something this morning!" Ralph said, picking up on what was going on.

"Too excited . . . I . . . I . . ." Persephone dropped to the ground in what appeared to be a dead faint. There was a collective gasp from the crowd, and Gary Beard was distracted for a moment.

That was just enough time for Bram's skillful hand to dart out and snatch two of the envelopes in the box. Unfortunately, Gary Beard had skills of his own. Before Bram could pull his hand back, Gary Beard had grabbed his wrist and shook it.

"You're kidding me, right?" Gary Beard snorted. "Security! Please escort this group to the exit!"

Jandia whirled around, her sword in her hand, her eyes shining. Clearly she was ready for a fight.

"Look, the last thing we need right now is to get ourselves arrested," said Noel to Jojo. They both rushed to calm Jandia down as rent-a-cops descended. Even though they were a head shorter than Jandia and Mirak, the guards had walkie-talkies and could probably call on hotel security.

"What happened back there?" asked Bram as the group was hustled out of the ballroom. "I have grabbed purses five times larger than those envelopes without anyone seeing."

Noel looked up. "Maybe someone up there rolled for a dexterity check and got a low number."

"I wish you wouldn't say things like that," Ralph said. "It's a little too freaky to think about."

The security guards deposited them at the elevator banks. The biggest one took photos of them with his camera. "Any more trouble and we're calling the police," he warned.

"So what do we do now?" whimpered Cammi. "Have we lost already?"

"We haven't lost anything," Ralph said. "We need a plan."

Gerontius had been quietly observing all this, staying back. He was his usual calm and unruffled self. "Arpy, tell me: if this was a game, and you needed to get through those doors, what would you do?"

Ralph thought for a moment. "I guess . . . I'd look and see if there was another way into that room."

Gerontius nodded. "So would I. Let us proceed."

They moved away from the elevators and went down a hallway marked with an Exit sign.

As they reached the end of the hall, Mirak's eyes lit up. "Pray, is that what I think it is?" She gestured to the wall beside the last door on the left. There was a glass frame attached to it, and underneath the glass was a piece of paper. On the paper was a diagram.

Gerontius broke into a small smile. "If I am not mistaken, that is a map."

Noel peered at it. "It is! It's perfect!"

Torgrim looked closely. He tapped the glass. "What is that large area there?"

"It's the inner ballroom," Noel said excitedly. "This door leads down to the basement area. It's how they load big things like pianos and stuff into it."

"So if you follow the map, it should lead you to a door directly under the main stage," Ralph added, tracing it with his finger.

"We can meet you in there!" said Jojo, her eyes gleaming.

"Is it guarded by any monsters?" Jandia asked hopefully.

"Maybe a few," Persephone said.

Ralph stared at her.

"She wants to fight a monster so badly, I didn't want to disappoint her," Persephone whispered.

Mirak used her strong fingernails to try to pry the frame loose. It held tight. "Now, how to take the map with us?" she asked.

"The frame seems to be glued to the wall, and I bet the glass is shatterproof," said Cammi mournfully.

Torgrim stepped forward and raised his hammer. "We shall see about that."

"Wait!" Ralph shouted. "We don't want to damage anything! No one should know we were here."

Gerontius arched an eyebrow. "Young mistress Johnna. I seem to recall your magic box has the power to take and hold images within it?"

Jojo laughed. "Of course it does." She held up her phone and snapped a picture of it. "That was an easy one."

"Now all we have to do is get you guys down those stairs," Ralph said. He tried the door. It was locked, of course.

"Now what?" said Jojo.

"I will break the door with my hammer," announced Torgrim.

"I wouldn't do that," said Ralph.

"Why not?" asked Mirak. "He breaks doors down all the time."

"I know," Ralph said, thinking of all the dungeons and castles he'd gotten into in the game using Torgrim's Magic Hammer spell. "But I think the noise would call attention to us. And that's not what we need right now."

"So we're stuck," Cammi said, and sat down on the floor.

Ralph peered at the lock. It was a regular key lock, not one that needed a card. This was obviously from when the hotel was first built and hadn't been fitted with the newer locks.

Bram cocked his head and looked at Persephone's hair. "That's quite a complicated braid, my little rogue. How do you keep it in place, if you don't mind my asking?"

Persephone turned pink. "It's not that complicated, but you do need hairpins."

"Ah, just as I thought!" the halfling said. "Could I trouble you for one of them?"

Persephone reached behind her head and tugged. She handed a metal hairpin to Bram, who looked delighted.

Ralph nodded. He knew exactly what a rogue could do with a pin like that. But that was in the other world. "Do you really think you can use that to—"

Before he could finish the sentence, Bram had inserted the pin into the lock of the door handle, twisted a few times, and turned the handle. It opened. He turned to the others and bowed.

"You've got to teach me that," Noel said as he passed Bram to head down the stairs. One by one, they went into the darkness. Ralph peered in.

"I don't suppose there are any torches about?" asked Mirak hopefully.

Cammi, Persephone, and Noel all reached for their phones and turned on the flashlight function. The stairwell was filled with beams of light.

"Shouldn't we look for a light switch?" asked Jojo.

"I think you should leave it dark if possible," Ralph reasoned, "just in case security comes around. Or if someone else comes down to use the stairs. This way they'll have to switch on the lights and you'll know they're coming."

Nine heads nodded, lit from below by the lights from their phones.

Gerontius shook his head. "Such useful items. Would that we had such magic in our world."

They headed to the basement. Ralph looked after them. "I'll see you inside!" he said, and closed the door. He checked it, and the locking mechanism had reset.

Ralph reached into his pocket and looked at the golden twenty-sided die. His friends would be making their way through darkened tunnels, but he had an adventure of his own to complete. He headed back to the ballroom to meet it.

40

THE FELLOWSHIP OF THE DICE

Ralph walked quickly by the registration desk, avoiding Gary Beard, who was surrounded by an admiring group of staff, busy retelling the story of the insane cosplayers who almost stole membership badges and his bravery in calling security.

When he reached the door, Ralph flashed his badge to the security person, who nodded and let him pass. He checked his watch—ten minutes to noon. He would need to find the Mages of the Midwest soon. And hope it was somewhere close to where his friends were going to emerge.

He quickly scanned the enormous high-ceilinged ballroom. Tables of merchandise lined the outer walls, and a second row filled in the center. He passed by tables laden with the kind of things he normally could have spent hours happily enthralled in. There were meticulously crafted miniatures of various character types typical of Reign of Dragons at one table. Nearby, someone had constructed glorious three-dimensional maps of dungeons and castles and taverns, with fireplaces and tiny torches that lit up, all for sale.

Ralph passed tables of T-shirts with corny slogans like ASK ME ABOUT MY CHARISMA SCORE and THAT'S JUST THE WAY WE ROLL.

On other tables people were selling their own adventure modules, stories you could use with your group. It seemed like anything you could want related to Reign of Dragons was here. Someone was even selling fake swords and shields and amulets, to help those who liked to dress up as their character.

At the end of the long line of tables, Ralph stopped. The person manning the last table was dressed as a fearsome orc, with blood streaming down his disgusting jaws. The fact that the orc was presently pouring the remains of a bag of corn chips down his or her throat took away some of the effect.

Just as Ralph was about to ask where he could find the Mages of the Midwest area, he looked straight ahead and laughed out loud.

It was hard to miss. At the very end of the ballroom, there were a few hundred seats set up, facing a raised stage. On the stage was a huge sign with the logo for Mages of the Midwest, a dragon seated upon a giant golden bejeweled throne.

On the far left side of the stage were seven chairs. On the far right was a small lectern with a microphone. What was in the middle, however, was what caused Ralph to gasp out loud.

They had built a perfect scale model of the Komach'Kreel. Standing over twelve feet tall, the monster looked even more fearsome than Ralph had pictured it. Its face was frozen in a snarl, its crimson eyes open in fury, and its tail pulled back as if ready to strike. Making it must have cost a fortune.

"Please take your seats, as the ceremony is about to begin," a voice said from the lectern, and Ralph noted that most of the seats were already filled. There were kids his age with their dads, lots of young people in their twenties, and, scattered among them, more than a few gray-haired older guys, with more than a few ponytails. Every ten seats or so he spotted someone dressed as their character.

Ralph took one of the few remaining seats and wondered where the adventurers were. Had they gotten lost? They had a map, it was true, but he knew from the game that one wrong turn could waste valuable time.

"Welcome to RoDCon! We are so thrilled to have you!" said the man at the microphone. Ralph squinted and realized it was the man in the picture on the website.

"For those who haven't met me, I'm Andy Wycroft, and yes, my dad, Warwick, was the man responsible for creating Reign of Dragons."

A huge cheer went up from the crowd. Andy bowed. He was a part of history. Anyone who knew about the game knew that he'd been one of the very first players when his father was developing it. Unlike the casually dressed audience, he was in an elegant black suit, which was beautifully tailored to his slim frame. He had the same high forehead as his father, and jet-black hair, combed stylishly back, with a matching goatee.

"I am so pleased to be here for such an awesome celebration. The special fortieth-anniversary edition of the Search for the Seven Serpent Scepter module was a huge success, selling more than three million copies worldwide."

More cheers interrupted Andy. He pumped his fist in the air. Ralph looked around. The others should have been here by now.

"Now, as you know, this campaign historically has been impossible to finish," Andy continued. "What with everyone ending up meeting . . . who, again?"

Laughter from the audience.

Andy then gestured toward the giant statue behind him. "Oh, yes. Say hello to my little friend!"

More laughter and applause. Andy consulted a list in his hands. "Now we come to the reason we've gathered. To meet those game masters intrepid enough to have guided their forces all the way into the Temple of Kamach'Ldar and gathered the first six serpents. Each of these masters was sent a golden die, and we are happy to say that all of them appear to be here."

Andy peered out into the audience. "Would they please come up onstage and take their places as I call their names?"

Ralph hadn't really thought about a ceremony. He hoped it wouldn't be too embarrassing.

"Kerry Bremen, please come up!"

A pale, skinny teenager climbed onto the stage to the whoops of his friends. He must be a local, Ralph decided, to have his posse with him.

"Douglas Hamilton . . . Fumio Harikawa . . . Octavi Navarro . . . Marcus Cooper . . ."

As the men of different ages got up, it was clear this was an international group. Mages of the Midwest had spared no expense. Andy was down to the last two names.

"Declan Rogers . . ."

Ralph could barely believe it. Declan? Here?

"And Ralph Ginzberg! Please come up and join us!"

Ralph felt a flush in his cheeks as he walked up the aisle to the last remaining seat. He was given a tremendous high five from Declan.

Over the applause of the crowd, Declan turned to him a

huge smile on his face. "Dude! RPG! I should have guessed I'd see you up here! This is amazing, right?"

"Unbelievable," Ralph said, meaning it.

"Gentlemen, please bring your golden dice one at a time up to the altar," Andy said.

Now that he was onstage, Ralph could see that there was a small oval table directly under the statue. There were seven small indentations in the table, each one meant for one die.

"We will start with the d4 die, followed by the d6, d8, d10, the percentile d10 . . ."

As each die was called, the person holding it came up and placed it carefully in its proper place on the altar. Declan had the d12 and went up. That left Ralph.

Andy turned to him. "Finally, the young man with the golden d20."

As he crossed the stage and went to the altar, Ralph had the oddest sensation. The die in his hand had started to glow. He held it tightly and felt it getting hotter and hotter the closer it came to the other dice, and it felt as if it were pulling him toward it.

He stood before the altar and paused.

He looked over at Andy, who was staring at the glowing die in his hand.

"What are you waiting for?" Andy hissed. "Put it where it belongs."

Ralph looked at the die. It was now almost too hot to hold.

Then two things suddenly happened, one after the other.

First a man stood up in the audience. "Do not put that with the others!" the man commanded.

Ralph noted with a start that he had seen the man before. It was the beggar from State Street.

"You're too late!" said Andy as he grabbed the die from Ralph's hand. Just then, a crashing noise was heard from somewhere behind the statue on the stage. All heads turned to see a trapdoor being smashed open by a hammer from below. Out sprang Torgrim, followed by Jandia, Gerontius, and Mirak, with Ralph's four friends taking up the rear.

A murmur went up through the crowd, and then applause. They obviously thought this was part of the show.

Ralph turned to look at Andy, who didn't seem the slightest bit surprised to see the interlopers.

"Well, you certainly took your time," Andy said easily.

Jandia saw the Komach'Krèel and quickly drew her sword.

"Stay your blade," Gerontius said. "It is but a statue."

Torgrim and Bram were arguing. "If you'd had a small dram of patience, Cleric, I would have had that lock."

The wizard was oblivious, his gray eyes locked on Andy. He stood stock-still, as if in shock.

"And if I had four hooves and a mane, I'd be a stallion," grunted the dwarf. "You were taking forever, and we needed to get here."

Mirak pushed past them and joined Gerontius at the front of the stage. She turned pale at the sight of Andy.

"Lord Andromodus! Here?"

As Andy bowed, Ralph began to put things together.

Andy.

Short for Andromodus.

41

ROLL FOR COMBAT

Andy, or Andromodus, gave a polite bow. "I am so glad to see you again, my loyal subjects." He held out his hand. "I believe you have certain objects I requested that you bring me."

"I think not," Gerontius said. He turned and looked to the old beggar, who had come to the foot of the stage. "Good sir, I suspect you are the cause of our being here. For what purpose?"

Before the man could answer, Ralph stepped toward him. "You . . . you're Warwick Wycroft, aren't you?"

A murmur went through the audience, along with scattered applause, as the adventurers turned and stared at Wycroft, wide-eyed.

"The Wizard Wycroft! It cannot be!" gasped Torgrim, going down on one knee.

"What sorcery is this?" exclaimed Gerontius.

Declan looked confused as he and the other GMs scrambled off the stage.

"Get out of here, humans!" Andromodus said.

Wycroft sighed. "I wish you'd stop talking like that, Andy. You're human too!"

"Not for long, Father!" Andromodus said. "And stop calling me Andy! I am Andromodus, wizard of the highest level! You said so yourself!"

"In the game, Andy," Wycroft said. "Now stop this nonsense."

"We shall see what nonsense it is when I have brought together all seven serpents!" said Andy. "My power is greater than you think! After thirty years, an adventuring force has finally found the hidden serpent."

Ralph turned to Andy. "What hidden serpent? What are you talking about?"

"I was afraid of this," Wycroft said. "It is no good, Andy. You cannot control the scepter."

"I am the one who summoned them to this world!" snarled Andromodus. "And I didn't even need to bring them to me. You did that!"

"Yes, I did," Wycroft said. "But not to help you. To call you out and to fight you once and for all."

"They cannot fight me," Andy said. "Once I have the serpent in hand . . ."

Ralph was frantically scanning the room. The Golden Serpent had to be here somewhere. If he could get to it . . . It must have something to do with the dice.

Bram stepped forward. "Good Andromodus, you are quite mistaken. We do not have the serpents with us. Sadly, we have left them in the temple. If you wish to send us back to retrieve them—"

"You lie, Rogue!" Andromodus said. "Look!"

The pockets of Gerontius's cloak and robe were moving as if being pulled by invisible hands. He muttered something under his breath and gestured with his arms. This did nothing. The wizard looked as if he were being dragged toward the altar.

"The six serpents seek their sister," Andy said in triumph.

"That's a mouthful!" said Noel. "Try saying that five times fast!"

"Shut up. This is serious!" Jojo said.

"You see, Father? Their spells are useless here."

"You still have your swords!" Persephone called out.

Jandia charged forward, and then suddenly the oddest thing happened. She seemed to hit some sort of hard barrier before reaching Andy, who stood, impassive.

"One of your earliest spells, Father. I believe the Barrier of Safety was in the first edition of the game," Andromodus laughed.

Gerontius was almost at the altar.

Ralph knew he had to do something. He thought of the golden d20; the twenty-sided charm had summoned the heroes to this world. There it was, glowing on the altar.

Transfixed, Ralph grabbed the die.

The room began to hum.

Andy whirled around. "Don't do that! Do not play with things you do not understand!"

"Go for it!" yelled Noel.

"I hope this works," Cammi whispered.

Ralph thought what he should ask for. "I roll for return of powers," he declared. The die rolled onto the altar, with the number 20 faceup. A critical hit. The hum was now deafening. The people in the audience were holding their ears. The stage began to rumble. There was a peal of thunder.

"You little brat! I hate you!" wailed Andy.

"He has unleashed the old magic!" said Warwick, smiling.

Gerontius fell back. He pulled his orb out of one of his sleeves. It was practically jumping from his hand, bright red beams shooting out from its center.

Torgrim intoned, "I call upon my god to smite the enemy's defenses."

A crackling bolt of energy shot from his hammer and surrounded Andy. There was a shattering noise as the barrier was breached.

Jandia moved forward with a snarl. "For those of my tribe who died at your hands!"

Mirak joined her, bow in hand, arrow nocked. "For all of Demos!"

Andy sighed. "You thought I would not have prepared for this?" He moved toward the altar and grabbed the d20.

"Now I believe it is my turn!" said Andy, throwing it on the table. "For I am the game master here! Roll for awakening!"

He threw the dice down, and it rolled slowly, finally landing faceup on 5. Andy bumped the table, and the die hopped up and landed on 20.

"That's cheating!" said Noel.

"I play by my own rules!" Andy answered, stepping back.

Ralph felt a sickening sensation as the floor began to wave and buckle, throwing him and his friends off their feet. He looked up to see what was causing this.

He was staring into the eyes of the Komach'Kreel, which was slowly coming to life.

Before he could stop himself, Ralph cried out. "What sorcery is this?"

42

THE END OF THE CAMPAIGN

The great beast hissed, an ugly, terrifying sound. Ralph tried to catch his breath as the Komach'Kreel whirled around, sniffing the air. As he turned, great sizzling streams of drool escaped his jaws.

Ralph felt a stinging sensation on his arm. He looked down and saw where one of the droplets had landed, burning his skin.

Through the pain, he realized what had to be done. Grabbing the d20, he threw it to Cammi. No team of adventurers had ever defeated a Komach'Kreel. How would this end?

Ralph turned to Gerontius. "Cammi needs to roll for you. We will use the portal to send you back to your world."

"No, we will not leave you to this!"

Bram looked at Ralph. "If we cannot defeat him in our world, then we must in this one!"

"Roll it!" Ralph commanded. Cammi paused for a moment, then nodded. He looked at Gerontius.

"Gerontius casts a spell of divine fire," he intoned, and rolled the die.

Gerontius whirled and placed his hands in front of him. Beams of fire like energy sprang from his palms and hit the creature square in the chest, pushing him back. Dazed, the Komach'Kreel shook his head to clear it. Before Andy could reach him, Cammi had passed the die back to Ralph, who didn't hesitate.

"Protective Shield of Greater Good!" he yelled as he rolled, and Torgrim, already holding his amulet, chanted the phrase with him.

The great barbed tail of the monster swung around, knocking the dais off the stage. As it approached the group, it bounced off the invisible barrier, leaving no damage.

Andy cursed and pounded on the shield. Out of the corner of his eye, Ralph saw Warwick point at his son. Andy froze and then fell senseless to the ground. "I think you've made enough trouble for one day," Warwick called as he joined the fighters onstage.

Noel tapped Ralph on the shoulder. He was with Bram, and both were grinning. "Our turn!"

"Roll for stealthy strike," Noel said, throwing the die on the altar. It showed a 17.

As the barrier dissolved, Bram tucked and rolled directly under the creature's legs, bringing him face to face with its plated underbelly. He looked out for guidance. Warwick yelled to him. "He has one weakness. There is a small space between the third and fourth plates!"

"Now you tell us!" yelled one of the GMs from the audience. Clearly they all still thought this was part of the event.

"I had to keep a few things out of the book." The old man winked.

The Komach'Kreel opened its jaws and released a stream of fire, which missed the group by a hair.

"What's taking you so long, you infernal rogue!" yelled Torgrim.

"Is it third from the tail or from the front?" asked Bram, counting furiously while trying to avoid being spotted by the monster.

"You know, I don't recall," said Warwick.

Ralph handed him the die. "Memory check."

Jandia had had enough. "I will not let some die decide my fate. I go NOW!" It was clear that Jandia was going to rely on her own strength.

Jojo grabbed her arm, and Jandia turned to face her. Jojo let out a small yelp. Jandia's eyes had turned a terrifying shade of red. As Jojo knew, this was the bloodrage, and once the barbarian went there, she would have to taste blood. She immediately released her grip on Jandia, who with a fierce bellow turned to charge the beast.

By this time, Warwick had rolled. It was a 15. He brightened. "Ah, yes. Third from the tail end. The slightly purple one."

Jandia was swinging her sword at the Komach'Kreel, which clawed at her with its giant forelegs. She dodged the first two attempts, but as she raised her sword, the beast knocked her down with a sideways blow. She lay stunned and helpless as the creature reared back to deliver the death blow.

All of a sudden, it screamed in pain. Arching its back, it let out another howl. Salt and Pepper had found their marks.

Jandia, breathing hard, was still lying prone on the floor.

There was no time to lose. Jojo rolled a 12. "Jandia uses the thrust with a strength of ten," she yelled.

Wincing in pain, Jandia twisted her body and swung the massive blade around, cutting one of the legs of the Komach'Kreel cleanly off. The monster toppled to the floor.

Mirak and Penelope turned to Warwick. "Is there something else you have not put in your books?" Persephone asked.

"Yes, I suppose there is. But it requires the creature to be at lower health than he is now," he said, scratching his chin.

Jandia had pulled out her sword and aimed for the neck of the creature. Raising her blade high, she brought it down onto the creature, who shrieked as her blade hit its mark.

From the side, there came another sound, an insistent thrumming rhythm, as Mirak began to strum her harp. Persephone had rolled an 18. The bard let out a long cry, both musical and strange, which agonized the creature. It looked up, dazed, trying to locate the source of the terrible music that tortured it.

As it writhed and turned, Ralph could see that the great ugly yellow eyes were dimming.

"Ah," said Warwick, stepping forward. "I do believe its health is quite low now." He retrieved the die from where Persephone had rolled it and intoned, "Banishment to the Abyss!" He rolled, and his eyes lit up. "Well, what do you know? A twenty! A critical hit!" He turned to Ralph. "You know, I haven't played in ages. I forgot how much fun it is."

Ralph wasn't paying attention to what was being said, his eyes glued to the back wall of the ballroom. It seemed to melt, dissolving into some sort of dark and deep blackness, which pulled the creature toward it.

Bram ran over to the creature and hopped on its belly.

"What in the name of Mora do you think you're doing?" shouted Torgrim.

"Salt and Pepper!" the halfling called. He was tugging at them, trying to pry them from between the plates in the belly where they were lodged.

"We will buy you a dozen knives!" pleaded Mirak. "Abandon these or be swept into the Abyss!"

Torgrim crouched down and took a deep breath.

Bram looked up. "Why, it is getting awfully close," he called back cheerfully. Torgrim launched himself at Bram's legs, holding on with all his might against the pull of the oncoming darkness.

"You will not leave us this way, Rogue!" he muttered.

With one final tug, the knives popped out, and the halfling and the dwarf tumbled onto the stage, just as the Komach'Kreel fell into the pit leading to the place of the Eternal Void. The back wall reappeared as if nothing had happened.

There was a moment of silence as the children and the heroes caught their breath.

Then the room burst into applause.

43

A STORY IS TOLD,
AND FAREWELLS ARE MADE

The fire department had been called, and the guests of the convention were filing out. Gary Beard kept apologizing to Ralph and the others, saying if he'd known they were the performers he wouldn't have treated them like that, and why didn't they say anything?

Declan had brought up his own RoD group to meet the kids and the heroes.

"That was fantastic," a tall young man with a fuzzy ringlet of hair and a long neck told Ralph and Noel. "You guys were so believable."

"I couldn't help but overhear," said Persephone, joining the boys. "Did you really like the performance?"

"Absolutely!" another of Declan's crew chimed in, a short, squat guy wearing horn-rimmed glasses and a MAY ALL YOUR HITS BE CRITICAL T-shirt. "And the special effects were phenomenal!"

"Would you like me to autograph your badge?" asked Persephone.

"Um, that's okay," the taller one said, backing away.

As they turned to go, Persephone overheard the smaller one say, "Actually, I thought she was kind of overacting at the end. . . ."

The taller guy nodded. "Totally."

"Hey!" Persephone yelled after them. "I was NOT OVER-ACTING!" She crossed her arms and turned to see Mirak smiling at her.

"We have a saying in my home village," Mirak said. "'Even the lowly sparrow wants to teach the songbird how to sing.'"

"Yeah, we just say, 'Everybody's a critic,'" said Persephone with a pout.

The group had moved from the hotel to a small restaurant nearby. Warwick joined them, with the revived Andy, who looked stunned at the unexpected turn of events.

"It was all mine," he kept saying to himself. "The power . . . I would have been known and feared throughout all Demos. . . ."

Warwick patted his wrist. "Shush, now, Andy. Listen, do you want a grilled-cheese sandwich? Or how about some chicken?" He had ordered ribs and chicken by the pound for the whole table.

Jandia was tearing into half a roast chicken as Torgrim finished tending to her wounds.

He turned to Ralph. "Come on, young one. Let me see your arm."

In the rush and excitement of all that had happened, Ralph had almost forgotten the burn on his arm. But he had to admit that as they walked over to the restaurant, the throbbing had become almost unbearable.

Ralph winced in pain as Torgrim grasped his arm with his big hairy hand. The cleric closed his eyes and recited a silent prayer.

It was astonishing. As the prayer continued, it was as if Torgrim were pulling out all the hurt. Finally, the dwarf removed his hand. No trace of an injury remained.

"There," Torgrim said with a kind look in his eye. "All better."

Noel nodded, impressed. And then he couldn't resist. "At least he didn't kiss your boo-boo."

Torgrim looked irritated. "Is that some sort of expression for something untoward? Because I'll have you know, you little—"

"No!" Ralph assured him. "It's what your mother does when you're a kid."

Torgrim gave them both a look that suggested he didn't completely believe them.

Noel's eyes widened as he looked at Torgrim. "Dude. You've changed. . . ."

"If this is one of your little games, Noel," Torgrim sputtered.

"Torgrim. Look," Ralph said softly, holding up his phone with the selfie camera on.

The dwarf peered at the phone. Staring back at him was his face. There was definitely something new about his appearance, although it was hard to decide just what.

"I can feel it. My soul is healed. But . . . but how?" he stammered.

"Remember how you had to perform one selfless deed to lift the curse?" Ralph asked. "Well, during the battle—"

"You risked your own life to save Bram from falling into the Abyss with the monster!" Noel had to jump in.

Ralph glared at him. "Let's face it, you were going to take too long telling it," Noel said simply.

"My fellow travelers, look upon me!" Torgrim called out to his friends. "I am healed!"

"You are indeed!" said Mirak. "Both inside and out!"

"Now I shall have my choice of dwarvish maidens!" Torgrim exclaimed happily.

Bram and Jandia exchanged glances.

"What?" asked Torgrim.

"You still aren't exactly the pick of the litter, if you get my meaning," Bram said.

"Hmph," snorted Torgrim. "What do you know? Rogues never tell the truth."

Noel had gone to sit by Warwick. "I still don't understand why Andy summoned the adventurers here."

"Do you wish to tell them, son?" Warwick asked Andy, who glowered at him and said nothing.

"It goes back to the start of RoD," Warwick began, taking a bite of his grilled-cheese sandwich. "It has been part of the history of the game that I am its inventor. This is not exactly true."

Ralph gazed at the old man, and suddenly it all became clear. "You're . . . you're not of this world, are you?" he asked, his voice hardly more than a whisper. "You're the last wizard. The one who divided the scepter."

Warwick closed his eyes and took a breath. Everyone at

the table was now listening. "Yes, Ralph, that is correct. But that is literally ancient history." He gave a small smile. "I did that without consulting the spirits of my fellow wizards. As punishment, the Old Ones banished me to this world, giving me a chance to make something of myself in a world without magic. All I had were my spellbooks, and knowledge and skills that did me little good.

"I met Andy's mother and tried to do all sorts of things. I failed at every one. In time, my memories of my home world began to fade. So I created Reign of Dragons in order to remember them. I told tales of my adventures to Andy and his friends—"

"And one of those kids' dads was the guy who invested in making the game and became your partner, and tried to take the game away from you—OW!" Noel cut in.

Jojo had poked him in the arm with a fork. Jandia gave her an approving look.

"I read the official history of Reign of Dragons like a hundred times," Noel said, looking sheepish.

"Don't mind him," Persephone said. "We want to hear it from you."

"I had told Andy and his friends mostly the truth, at least where the scepter was concerned," Warwick continued.

"Not the whole truth," Andy sniped. His arms were crossed, and he was pouting.

"I could not trust you with the whole truth. I put a false fifth scepter in the published adventure so that you would never know."

Andy glared at his father. "You could have shared it with me once I found your spellbooks and discovered your secret."

"Andy, my son. I tried to help you." Warwick turned back to the others. "I had brought the last of the serpents, the Golden Serpent of power, with me as one last precaution so that no one in Demos could ever collect all seven. Then came the day when Andy begged me to send him to my home world. He had never been able to come out from behind my shadow, so I felt I owed him this. There was still enough magic in the one serpent, and he was not banished, as I was."

Gerontius leaned in. "This is where you became Andromodus, ruler of all Athanos."

Andy smiled at the memory. "Here on earth I was a nobody. The son of the great Warwick Wycroft, creator of the beloved Reign of Dragons. But on Demos, I was king. I had a court and was able to send out countless adventurers to search for the serpents of the scepter."

"Was ruling Athanos not enough?" asked Mirak, shaking her head.

Persephone nodded in agreement. "You got what you wanted."

Warwick sighed. "For some, like Andy, there is never enough."

Andy waved his hand dismissively. "What I wanted was to be the True King of all Demos. For this, I needed the scepter."

"Ultimately, I waited until at last the true fifth serpent was revealed. For thirty years, I had watched as groups playing the game found the bone serpent of the kobold's rib, which we all thought was the one they needed."

Ralph remembered that from the story. He didn't dare look at Persephone.

"Only when that girl set her bard to the challenge of the minstrel's was the true serpent revealed."

Persephone looked like she was going to burst.

Ralph sighed. "All right, Persephone, say it."

"It was my story! The one you all hated!"

"I didn't hate it," said Cammi. "I thought it was cool, re-member?"

"The point is, the moment she stumbled on the true ser-pent by discovering the flute-shaped serpent, I could feel it. It was time to return to the world of my birth and claim the Golden Serpent from my father." Andy's mouth was set in a tight line. "But he had disappeared, having sold the company years earlier. He had feared this day might come. He had melted the Golden Serpent down—"

"Into a set of dice!" Jojo exclaimed. Noel tried to poke her with a fork, but she parried with a butter knife and knocked the fork out of his hand.

Jandia beamed.

Warwick hadn't taken his eyes off his son the whole time he was telling the story. "I thought I was being so careful. I kept an eye on who had reached the end of the adventure, and that's when I sent the dice out to the different game masters."

"You had to bring the group with the Serpent Flute into our world," Ralph said to Andy.

"It was tricky to come up with a spell to add that last page to your notes," Andy replied, "but I knew once you had it, you would use the portal and the die would take care of the rest. I had already rejoined the Mages of the Midwest, who were delighted to have a Wycroft associated with the product."

"All you needed to do was come up with a way to gather all the dice in one place," said Cammi.

"It wasn't easy to convince the company to bring you

together to celebrate the fortieth anniversary of the Serpent Module, but once I did . . ."

"You would have gotten away with it, too, if it hadn't been for us meddling kids!" said Noel.

"Something like that," muttered Andy.

Noel turned to Gerontius. "That's from a famous cartoon show. That's why it's funny."

Gerontius nodded politely. Cammi whispered to him, "I'll explain it later."

"There's still something I don't understand," said Noel, always one for logic. "You just created the game, not the world. How did the characters we created end up there? That makes, like, no sense."

Warwick nodded in approval. "That's a very good question, young man. Although I should have hoped that by now sense would be the last thing you would rely on when it comes to my story. The truth is that the world I come from possesses deep magic, and it hated the chaos and uncertainty that splitting up the seven serpents caused."

All five of the kids were hanging on his every word. The old mage reached for a rib. "These look extremely good."

"Mr. Wycroft, please!"

"Ah yes. The world. When someone played the Seven Serpents story, it actually called the characters you created to Demos, and they existed there to find and bring together the pieces of the scepter. The poor people of Demos were cursed to repeat the same days over and over again, until someone as clever as young Phoebe here found the answer to my little puzzle."

Persephone was so enrapt, she didn't even correct him.

"As each new group of adventurers joined the game, they would sometimes run across other searchers, depending on the story their GM told," Warwick continued.

"Yes, I think that happened to us," Ralph said, thinking back to the nasty group they had encountered in BlackBriar, during Jojo's adventure.

"But that's all over now, thanks to you," Warwick said. "And to you," he called out to the adventurers, who were still busy eating. It seemed that as long as there was food in front of them, they were happy.

Warwick pushed away from the table and wiped his mouth on a napkin. Jojo watched as Jandia, who had been busy licking her fingers, noticed this. Jandia carefully wiped her mouth on the tablecloth. Well, it was a start.

Warwick stood up. "I think we know what happened next. And now the story can finally come to its proper ending."

He swept out of the restaurant, and the others followed.

The group crossed the long six-lane street of Boerum Place, and Warwick headed to a modest park. There were small groves of trees surrounding a large playing field, where families and children with babysitters were playing Frisbee and soccer.

The old man led them past the field to a clearing between two groups of trees. It was deserted for the moment.

He held out his hand. "It is time to reunite the scepter. Please present the six serpents, one by one."

Gerontius bowed. "We must counsel first. I am sure you understand."

"Do as you must," said Wycroft.

Torgrim stroked his beard furiously as they stepped

away. "The scepter holds too much power. I'm not sure about this."

Mirak nodded. "For once, I agree with our cleric. How do we know that this is all true?"

Gerontius looked at Wycroft. "I think he does not lie. There is honor in him."

Bram spoke up. "Let us presume that all he says is right. Do we not deserve some sort of reward? Or perhaps we could keep the scepter for ourselves."

"I can kill them both if you like," Jandia said happily.

"No!" said Ralph. "You have to give him the serpents."

The adventurers turned to him and stared.

"You have certain wisdom for one so young, but you also have much to learn about the world," Torgrim said.

"*We* have a lot to learn?" said Jojo in exasperation. "Warwick may have created the scepter, but we created you, remember?"

That stopped the adventurers cold. They looked at one another, unsure of what to do.

Cammi went up to Gerontius and pulled at his robe. "Please. This is the way to get back to your world."

Gerontius nodded. He turned to Warwick. "We will do as you say. On the condition you send us back to our world."

"I will not send you back," Wycroft said.

Jandia let out a low growl and pulled out her sword.

"Sheathe your weapon," chuckled Wycroft. "I did not finish. I will not *send* you back. I will *take* you back."

"But you're banished!" said Ralph. "Aren't you?"

"I am old and can protect the scepter no more. Now that you have so bravely collected the serpents, I have pledged to the Old Ones to destroy it, and thus the banishment will be lifted. I will end my days as the Mage of Athanos."

Andy brightened. "And I will come too?"

Warwick shook his head. "No, Andy. You are cursed to live out your life here on your home world, a common man as well."

Andy's face fell. "But . . . that's not fair. . . ."

Noel snorted. "Dude, you tried to kill us with that Komach'Kreel and grasp ultimate power. Just be glad your dad doesn't, like, turn you into stone or something."

"Well said!" proclaimed Bram.

Warwick reached out his hand once again. "And now the time has come."

Gerontius stepped forward and took the first scepter from the sleeve of his robe. "The Iron Serpent, from the dungeon of Fahrenthold."

Torgrim reached into his chain mail and took out the second, which was hanging from a cord around his neck. "The Silver Serpent, from the Dragon Girl of Draakland."

Bram removed another from his boot. "And here is the Crystal Serpent, from the wand of the wizard Ragus of Kendzion."

Gerontius took the other from the spine of his spellbook. He looked at Cammi as he said, "And here is the Wooden Serpent from the Tree of Swords of Zwaardwood."

Jandia knelt down and pulled the fifth from her leather leg protector. "The Jade Serpent, from the mayor of the false village of Waterspout-on-Nyfitsa."

Mirak stepped forward. She shared a smile with Persephone as she undid her harp. There, in a hollowed area under the tuning pegs, was nestled the Bone Serpent.

"And here is the Serpent of Bone, the true serpent, won from Minstrel Chioni on the snowbound isle of Nivis," she said, and handed it to Wycroft.

The six serpents shimmered in the sunlight as a light wind began to whirl the leaves around them.

"The serpents wish to join together," Wycroft said. "It is time to say your farewells."

Persephone put her arms around Mirak, who stroked her hair. "Never forget there is great music in you," she whispered into the girl's ear.

"Are you kidding?" said Persephone. "I live to sing. I mean, singing is my life."

"It is also a gift to give others," said Mirak.

Noel turned to Bram; they had both overheard this. "Great," said Noel, "now we'll never get her to shut up."

Bram regarded Noel and thought for a moment. "You are a good, honest young man, you know?"

"Yeah, I guess so," said Noel. "Is that bad?"

"Well, it doesn't make for a good rogue, that's for certain," admitted Bram. "And perhaps you needn't be quite so honest all the time."

"I don't understand," Noel said. "Why would I lie?"

"To spare someone's feelings, I suppose," said Bram. "But that's for you to decide, my lad."

Jandia was standing uncomfortably with Jojo, whose chin was quivering. The barbarian peered at her. "Are you going to cry? A warrior does not cry."

"I don't want to," Jojo said, her voice cracking. "It's just that . . . I really liked hanging out with you."

Jandia looked away. "But this is weakness! When my family was slain, I did not cry. I swore an oath to drink the blood of my enemies."

Jojo wiped her face with her sleeve. "Well, that's great for you. I'm not a warrior. I'm a kid. And I'm sad that you're going. I'm sorry!"

Jandia looked at her for a moment. The ends of her mouth turned down. "Waaaah!" she wailed, and hugged Jojo.

"You're crushing me," Jojo said in a small voice.

"I am sorry," said Jandia, wiping away her tears. "I am done. We shall never speak of this."

"That's cool," Jojo said.

Gerontius pulled his robes around Cammi, who was hunched over. The wizard brought his head close to Cammi's and gazed at him. "I sense you hold great secrets inside you," he said quietly.

Cammi said nothing, but nodded.

"I know something of this, and please hear me. You are a beautiful and perfect person."

Cammi shook his head.

"Heed my words, human child," Gerontius persisted. "You need not fear anyone. You can do great things. And you will."

Cammi looked up, deep into the gray eyes of the elf wizard. "I wish I felt that way," he finally said.

"With time, you will," Gerontius said, smiling. "And if others do not see it, you will learn to laugh at them or fight them with your wit and your gifts."

Cammi shook his head again. "I want to go with you."

"Your place is here in this world. You will find it, Cammi. That is your destiny."

Torgrim was standing apart, with Ralph. "There is something heavy on your heart."

Ralph had been watching the others. Then he turned to Torgrim. "They say they no longer want to play the game," he said, looking at the ground. "What will become of you?"

"We will be whatever our fates have planned for us," Torgrim said simply. "Perhaps it is those dice that control them, or perhaps there is more in our world than can be contained in a simple game of children."

"I can't stand the thought of you just disappearing," Ralph said. "We've been together for years. How can they simply walk away?"

"There is a time for all things, life and death, and we cannot control them." Torgrim reached out and rested his hands on Ralph's shoulders. He pulled him in. "Young Arpy, take hold of the sacred amulet."

Ralph didn't want to do this, but it wasn't really a request. More like an order. He felt compelled to do as Torgrim said. He reached out and wrapped his fingers around the rude stone carved with ancient symbols. He could feel something coursing through him as he held it. It was healing something deeper than his arm. He felt at peace. Whatever would happen, would happen.

They turned to Warwick, who intoned, "Let those who would travel with me clasp hands and form a circle."

The kids stepped aside to let the adventurers join the old mage.

He lowered his head and began to recite an ancient spell. As he did, the serpents on the ground raised themselves, and as though invisible hands were solving an intricate puzzle, they fit themselves together, each linking with the others, forming a dazzling scepter. Finally, as the scepter raised itself to waist level, Wycroft reached into his pocket and took out the golden die, which shimmered in his hands, softening and melting as he formed it into a long, snakelike shape. When he was done, it leapt from his hands with a hiss and wrapped itself around the other six. The ground began to shake, and then everyone felt the familiar vibrations.

Suddenly, there was a strangled cry from Andy. "I will not be left behind!" he cried, and tried to break into the circle.

Wycroft sighed. "Oh, for heaven's sake, Andy. I do wish you'd stop this foolishness." He waved his hands, and again Andy fell to the ground, senseless.

"When he wakes, tell him his father loves him and to be a good boy," Wycroft called out over the whipping sounds of the portal opening into the other world, the world of magic and spells and adventures Ralph loved so much.

And then they were gone.

Jojo looked down at Andy.

"So who's going to tell him?"

Nobody said anything.

"How about we just leave him a note?" suggested Noel, taking a pad of paper and a pen from his pocket.

"Sounds good to me," said Ralph.

There was no argument.

44

THE END OF THE REIGN OF DRAGONS?

The kids still had the key cards, so they were able to collect their belongings from the hotel room. There was just enough money to leave a big tip for whoever would be cleaning up the mess left by their friends.

They walked out, taking turns pushing and pulling the dolly and the other stuff they'd borrowed from Ralph's parents. His friends decided to wait outside as he rang the bell.

As Ralph expected, his parents were not amused or understanding when he told them he'd used their equipment for a school science project. He had to endure a lecture about being respectful of other people's property and how would he like it if they took his stuff, like his laptop, for a week or two. The argument that they had missed his birthday didn't get a lot of traction.

They told him they would decide his punishment and let him know at dinner, but let him say goodbye to his friends.

"So how bad is it?" Jojo asked as he emerged from the house and joined them on the stoop.

"It could be worse," Ralph said.

"They sounded pretty mad," said Noel. Then he brightened. "Hey, look at this!" While the others had been on their phones, he had been passing the time rereading the Search for the Seven Serpents. "The last page has changed!"

He looked down at the page and read:

"'Upon the defeat of the Komach'Kreel, deliver the scepter to the aged Wizard Wycroft, who will reward you handsomely.'"

There was even an illustration. Five intrepid adventurers—a dwarf cleric, a barbarian warrior, an elf wizard, a halfling rogue, and a half-orc bard—were presenting the scepter to a very thin and gaunt mage, who now had the requisite long white beard.

Ralph smiled. If this was their last game, at least it would always be remembered.

There was a jingling noise. Jojo shifted nervously and checked her phone. "Listen, that was Joie. They're still at the Atlantic Center mall. I'm going to meet them." She took a brush out of her bag and began brushing her hair.

Cammi looked up from his phone at Persephone.

He turned to Ralph. "So it seems rehearsal is still going on and they really want us to come so we can get caught up."

"Sure," said Ralph. "Of course." He turned to Noel.

Before he could say anything, Noel stood up. "Hey, Jojo, I'll go to Atlantic Center with you. I just texted my parents and they said it's cool."

"Um, Noel, I'm not sure you want to come," Jojo said. "We're shopping for pajamas at, like, girls'-type stores. . . ."

Noel shook his head. "I just meant I'd go on the train with you. GameStore has the new World War II game I want to try out."

Ralph stood alone on his stoop.

"So this is it?" he said to no one in particular. "This is how it all ends?"

His four friends stopped on the sidewalk and faced him. He couldn't read their expressions. Even Persephone, who was usually so easy to figure out (or else she'd tell you), was impossible to decipher, with a small smile on her face.

"What were you guys talking about when I was inside?" Ralph asked. "Are we on for next week or not?"

"Hey, you never know," Noel replied. "Guess you'll have to wait and find out!"

EPILOGUE

The Great Throne Room of Athanos had undergone a dramatic change. Where once there was darkness, now there was light. The deep brown oaken panels that had lined the walls were now white birch, and the heavy velvet curtains that had hung over each window were now muslin, letting the sunshine stream in, forming pools of light that glowed throughout the chamber.

The courtiers had changed as well. They were dressed in pastel pinks and blues, to match their mood, which seemed to bubble up into the very air, a combination of happy voices and laughter.

All this seemed to be a reflection of the man on the throne, who lounged easily in a loose white robe, his gentle eyes taking in the scene with a serenity that came from deep within.

A messenger dressed in scarlet ran into the room, and conversation ceased. The young page knelt in front of the throne.

The man in the white robe leaned forward to hear the news, then leaned back and broke into a smile.

"Excellent! Let them come forward!" he said, clapping his hands.

A murmur went through the assembled court as a group entered the hall. They approached the throne with easy confidence and an air of purpose.

"Gerontius Darksbane, so good to see you!" called the man.

"Great Mage, we come at your bidding," the wizard said, and bowed.

"May you always be blessed in the eyes of Orach'T'char," intoned the dwarf cleric at his side.

"Good Master Torgrim," the mage said, nodding. "And I am delighted to see you, Mirak! I have missed your songs, mistress."

"Ever at your service, sir," replied Mirak the bard, her hand on her heart.

"And am I to assume you are no less happy to see me?" insisted the small person at her side, his arms crossed. "Or shall I take my leave?"

"Peace, Master Quickfoot," answered the mage. "Your skills and good company are as desired as those of any of your fellows."

The mage looked past the quartet. "But there seems to be one of your cohorts who is not present. I do hope no ill fate has overtaken her?"

Torgrim sighed and looked down. "We are at your command, Great Mage. There is no news of our brave and fearless comrade."

The mage looked pensive. Then he sighed. "Ah, well. The

gods have their reasons, have they not? What is important is that I have a task for which I needed the most intrepid, the most dauntless, the finest team of adventurers in all of Demos."

"Tell us our new task," said Bram excitedly, "and we will undertake it, no matter how challenging."

The mage cleared his throat, but before any words could leave his mouth, there was a commotion by the entrance. Someone was trying to push into the hall, strewing guardsmen left and right.

The imposing figure strode down the aisle toward the mage as the court erupted into gasps.

The red-maned warrior took her place next to the others.

"I am late, and that is unfortunate," she said.

"Jandia, you are right on time," said Gerontius happily.

Jandia Ravenhelm the Fearsome, Bane of the Kreel, turned to her comrades.

"Sorry. Gymnastics practice ran over."

"No problem," said Mirak, giving her a hug. "We're just glad you're here."

"Are you kidding?" said Bram. "She wouldn't have missed it for the world!"

"And now," said Torgrim, rubbing his hands together, "*alea iacta est*. The die is cast!"

THE END

ACKNOWLEDGMENTS

Every book is an adventure, both for the reader (hopefully) and especially for the author. This particular adventure began a few years ago, shortly after my son began playing Dungeons & Dragons with a group of friends. We were out walking one day and he turned to me and said, "Wouldn't it be cool if our characters came to life?" One is not often handed a gift like that, especially by your nine-year-old son, so to Jamie I say thanks.

Just like in the book, the group came together initially for Jamie's birthday, led by a tall, enthusiastic, patient, and imaginative Dungeon Master named Matt Weir. When Matt went off to grad school (just like in the book!), the kids did NOT take over. We were lucky enough to discover another brilliant Dungeon Master in the form of Vincent Eaton, whose passion for gaming and instilling that passion in others has been amazing to watch.

Since I never played D&D, the videos online by Dungeon Master extraordinaire Matthew Mercer for *Geek & Sundry,* especially his tutorials for aspiring DMs, were an invaluable resource. His three-hour sessions with his cohorts in the series *Critical Role* also helped me to get a feel for how a campaign moves forward week to week.

Of course, deepest and humblest thanks must go to original creators of D&D, Gary Gygax and David Arneson, along with all the others who helped develop this unique form of game play and storytelling; and to the good people at Wizards of the Coast, who allow other game makers to use the rules and basic character profiles of D&D to create their own RPGs (even my humble attempt here).

Thanks to my wife's nephew Sam Iwai's bookshelf, I discovered the extraordinary Dragonlance series of books, which helped me understand how to translate a D&D campaign into a literary adventure. A bow of respect to the authors, Margaret Weis and Tracy Hickman.

In the Professional Realm, I need to thank those brave and fearless warriors who have fought alongside me (and sometimes with me):

My agent, Holly Root, expert at casting the healing email spell;

My editor, Kate Sullivan, whose sword of truth and justice cuts through every passive voice and ungainly sentence;

Assistant to the editor, Alexandra Hightower, gatekeeper and winner of the Person Whose Name Is Most Likely to Appear in a Fantasy Novel award.

Once again, wizardly artist Octavi Navarro has created brilliant illustrations, with the invaluable aid of art director Katrina Damkoehler and designer Trish Parcell.

As always, my deepest gratitude goes to my supportive and loving parents, Bob and Joan Markell.

And continued appreciation to my mother-in-law, Alice Iwai, and father-in-law, Dr. Charles Iwai, and his wife, Sherry, for their warmth and unending good wishes.

To my big sister, Mariana Markell, and her husband, Jody Blanco, and their kids, Miranda, Max, and Peter (who aren't kids anymore!): a big hug and thank-you.

I have mentioned Sam Iwai above, but I need to mention his father, my brother-in-law, Jeff Iwai, and his wife, Wendy, and their other children, Nicholas and Emily. Without them life would be a whole lot less fun.

My own adventure would not be worth taking without my amazing wife, Melissa Iwai, at my side, sharing the ups and downs that every roll of the dice brings.

And finally, to the kids of the D&D group (past and present) that inspired this whole enterprise: Cole, Lila, Lucas, Marco, Max, Miles, Sam, Silas, and of course, my beloved Jamie.

READY FOR A DIFFERENT
KIND OF GAME?

Turn the page for a peek at Denis Markell's
first book, full of puzzles and mystery!

Excerpt copyright © 2016 by Denis Markell.
Published by Delacorte Press, an imprint of Random House Children's Books,
a division of Penguin Random House LLC, New York.

CHAPTER 1

WHO KNEW A MAN WITH TUBES IN HIS NOSE COULD BE FUNNY?

It looks like something from a science-fiction movie, with so many machines and tubes going into and out of bags hung on poles.

For a moment, it doesn't register that all those tubes and hoses are connected to a person.

I have no memory of what he looked like when I was little, and the only photo of Great-Uncle Ted in our house is from ages and ages ago. It shows a burly man with a crew cut, sitting in a living room in the 1960s. He's got a cigarette in one hand and a lighter in the other. I wonder if he hadn't smoked so many cigarettes maybe he wouldn't be here now. He's looking at the camera with a confident grin that says this is not a man to mess with. The only other place I've ever seen Asian men with kick-butt expressions like that is in samurai or martial-arts movies.

Not that I watch them all that much.

I mean, it's bad enough other people make assumptions about us Asian kids. No need for me to help out.

But I gotta say, that photo can't be further from the old man lying in this bed. The grossest thing is the tube going right up into his nose. It looks horrible, and is attached to a machine that does who knows what.

I go and stand awkwardly by the window, unsure of what to do. I wish Mom had come in with me, but she said Great-Uncle Ted wants to see me alone. Dying man's last wish and all, I guess. I clear my throat and sort of whisper, "Um, hi?"

"Arwhk."

The two veiny sacs of his eyelids slowly open, and when he sees me, he gestures, beckoning me over with one hand.

I gingerly approach the chair next to his bed, careful not to disturb any of the wires and tubes snaking around him. It's hard—I have visions of knocking into some hose or other just as I'm supposed to be having a nice visit.

"Gghhh . . ." Great-Uncle Ted catches my eye and reaches out.

Without thinking, I flinch. I have a flashback to a movie I saw where a guy laid out like this had a monster burst out of his chest and jump on someone's face. I'm not saying I expect that to happen here, but hey, it does go through my mind.

Great-Uncle Ted's eyes change. He points impatiently to something on the table.

A pad and paper. There is spidery writing on it.

"You want me to . . . give you the pad?" I ask.

Now there's a flash of fire in Great-Uncle Ted's eyes. I know when someone's ticked off. The message is clearly *Yes, you idiot. Give me the pad.*

I hand the pad to my great-uncle, who winces in pain as he presses a button on the side of his bed that raises him to a seated position.

Slowly, he writes something and then hands me the pad.

Hurts too much to talk. You Amanda's boy, Ted?

I start to write an answer on the pad.

The next thing I know, Great-Uncle Ted yanks the pad out of my hands. The old dude is surprisingly strong!

BEEP BEEP BEEP

Great. Now the heart-rate machine is going a lot faster. That can't be good.

He scribbles something and hands the pad back to me.

I'm not deaf, you little dope. Talk to me.

I laugh in spite of myself. Of course. Duh.

"Yes, uh, sir . . . I'm Ted." I feel a little weird introducing myself, since *he* knows who I am, but since I don't remember him, it feels like the right thing to do. And I'm pretty sure he seems like a "sir."

The old man writes some more. He's writing with more energy now.

You got big. Do you still like playing games?

"What games do you mean, sir?" I ask.

Kissing games.

What th—?

"Uh, no, sir," I begin. "I don't enjoy kissing games. That is, I've never played them. Maybe I would enjoy them if I did. I mean, you never know about something until you try it, right?" I'm babbling now. Trying to look casual, I lean against something, then realize it's a pole holding some fluid going into my great-uncle (or maybe coming out of him—hard to tell). Gross. I attempt to cross my legs, but I dare anyone to try to do it while wearing these ICU snot-green-colored clown pants they made me wear over my jeans to come in here. It's not so simple. So my leg sort of hovers half hoisted.

Meanwhile, Great-Uncle Ted is scribbling away.

I know you like computer games, you little twerp. I just wanted to see your face.

I laugh, and I see a hint of a smile under all the machinery.

You like the ones where you shoot people?

"I'm not allowed to play those," I say, which is the truth.

I didn't ask if you were allowed to. I asked if you liked them.

I smile and nod. This guy is pretty sharp. "Um . . . yeah, I play them sometimes."

Great-Uncle Ted looks at me with an expression I can't make out.

A lot of fun, huh?

"I guess." I shrug.

I hope that's the only way you ever have to shoot and kill a man. The other way is a lot less fun.

"You've killed a man?" I try to ask casually, but it kind of comes out in a squeak. Not my most macho moment, but give me a break, I wasn't ready for this.

Quite a few, yes.

What did Uncle Ted *do* before he retired? I wonder what sort of professions call for killing men. Or more precisely, "quite a few" men. Was he a soldier? A *hit man*?

Let's talk about something else. Why do you like these games so much?

I'm happy to move on. "I don't think the shooting games are all that—and that's the truth. It's more something to do with my friends when we hang out. What I really like is what are called escape-the-room games."

Tell me about them.

Sure, why not? "They're kind of puzzles, where you're stuck in a room and have to figure a way out."
Great-Uncle Ted's eyes survey the space around him.

There's only one way to escape this room.

"Well, I don't agree," I say eagerly, standing up to look around. "There are all sorts of exits, if you look carefully. Not just the door. There's that window. You could tie your sheets together and climb down there, or maybe there's an air-conditioning duct—"

TAP TAP TAP.

My brilliant analysis is interrupted by the sound of my great-uncle's pencil tapping loudly on the pad to get my attention.

I was actually referring to dying, Ted. Try to keep up.

I sit down, deflated. "I guess I didn't think of that," I say honestly, "because you seem so alive."

Great-Uncle Ted does his best to roll his eyes.

Don't bother sucking up to a dying man, Ted. You any good at these room games?

"Never seen a game I couldn't solve or beat. I'm always the top scorer—that means I've solved them quicker than anyone else. I guess that makes me the best," I say, before realizing how obnoxious it sounds. "That sounds like bragging. Sorry."

You ever heard of Dizzy Dean?

Okay, that's a little random. But old people do that sometimes. The name does sound kind of familiar, but I can't place it. I shake my head.

One of the best pitchers in the history of baseball.
When you go home, look up what he said about bragging.

Great-Uncle Ted settles back onto his pillow. He's clearly tired.

I stare out the window, watching the headlights of the traffic below making patterns on the ceiling. "Yeah. That's about the one thing I am good at," I say softly, almost to myself. I hear scratching, and he's up and writing more.

Don't ever sell yourself short, Ted. Your mother says you're
very smart.

I nod my head and laugh. "Yeah, I know, I just don't 'apply myself.' She's always saying that. Lila's the smart one."

Lila is my big sister, the bane of my existence. Lila the straight-A student, Lila the president of the student body. Lila, who got the highest Board scores in La Purisma High's history. Lila, who gave the most beautifully written senior address at her graduation, currently crushing it in her freshman year at Harvard. I mean, seriously. Why even try to compete with that?

Your mother told me you're smarter than your sister. You just
don't know it.

Oh, snap! I hope there's a burn unit at Harvard, because Lila just got *smoked.* Big-time!

I'm starting to like Great-Uncle Ted. But I feel bad. We've been talking about me the whole time I've been here. Well, except for the part about him killing a lot of people. I'm pretty sure I don't want to hear more about that.

"So I guess you knew my mom when she was a little kid," I begin. "What was she like?"

Amanda was a pain in the a

He stops and his eye drifts up to my face and back down to his pad.

Amanda was a pain in the a̶ behind, if you'll excuse my French.

I can't believe I thought this was going to be boring. This is *great*! "Seriously? How so?" It takes all the self-control I can muster to get this out without cracking up.

He writes for a long time, then hands the pad to me.

When she was nine, she had this thing where no matter what you would ask her she'd say, "That's for me to know and you to find out."
Like you'd ask her, "What flavor ice cream do you want?"
"That's for me to know and you to find out."
"What movie do you want to see?"
"That's for me to know and you to find out!"
"Do I have lung cancer?"
"That's for me to know and you to find out!"

I choke at that last one.

Great-Uncle Ted waves his hand wearily.

I made that last one up. But she did say it all the time. She thought it was cute. It stopped being cute after the first day. Then it was annoying as heck.

Great-Uncle Ted pauses.

But she was always smart. And I'm very proud of her.

Great-Uncle Ted was the one who paid for Mom to come to California from Hawaii and go to nursing school. She's been working here at La Purisma General Hospital for as long as I can remember.

Great-Uncle Ted looks up from the paper, and his wise, half-lidded eyes meet mine. He scrawls on the page and holds up the pad.

Please tell me about the games you play. How you solve these puzzles.

Wait. Is a real, live adult person actually asking me *details* about the games I play? This is unheard of.

So I go on and on, explaining how the games work, how at first nothing seems to make sense. But then, as I put my mind to it, a little click goes off in my head and the pieces begin to fit. It's an awesome feeling when it all comes together and you get it right.

Great-Uncle Ted seems genuinely interested, especially when I tell him about a particularly tricky puzzle, where if you look carefully at what appears to be a bunch of random drinking glasses on a tray, you realize they actually resemble the hands of a clock set to a particular time. Which is one of the main clues to solving that game.

"You know, maybe if they let me, I can come back tomorrow with my laptop and show you some," I'm saying, when I see that his head has fallen back onto the bed and his eyes are closed. "Great-Uncle Ted! Are you all right?" I gasp. "Should I get Mom?"

He wearily reaches for the pad and writes carefully.

I'm just tired. But I'm happy to see you again, Ted.

"I—I'm so glad I could talk to you too, sir," I say, feeling my breathing slow down again.

I feel so much better about everything now. You are ready.

Huh? What does that mean?

"That's good, sir."

The old man looks up at me. The energy is clearly draining out of him.

You must promise me one thing.

"I know, sir. I promise I'll work harder in school, and I'll never tell Mom you thought she was a pain in the behind—"

I think he'll laugh at this, but instead, he gathers his strength and writes furiously across the pad.

No! Listen to me! You must promise me

He's writing slower now, forcing the words out of the pen.

"Yes, sir?"

Great-Uncle Ted falls back and throws the pad at me.

THE BOX IS ONLY THE BEGINNING. KEEP LOOKING
FOR THE ANSWERS. ALWAYS GO FOR BROKE!
PROMISE ME!

With great effort, he tugs on my sleeve. I lean toward him. He pulls me down until my ear is close to his face. I can just make out the word he is saying.

"Promise!" the old man croaks. He releases my sleeve. He looks peaceful now, like a weight has been lifted off his shoulders.

As my great-uncle falls asleep, I hear my own voice, sounding far away, whispering, "I promise."

YEARLING

Turning children into readers for more than fifty years.

**Classic and award-winning literature for every shelf.
How many have you checked out?**

**Find the perfect book and meet your
favorite authors at RHCBooks.com!**